FOR HOPE
IS ALWAYS BORN

by
Jan Fortune

Liquorice Fish Books

L/FB 314

Published by Liquorice Fish Books, an imprint of Cinnamon Press,
Meirion House, Tanygrisiau, Blaenau Ffestiniog, Gwynedd, LL41 3SU
www.cinnamonpress.com

The right of Jan Fortune to be identified as author of this work has been asserted by herin accordance with the Copyright, Designs and Patent Act, 1988.

Copyright © 2019 Jan Fortune.

ISBN: 978-1-911540-07-6

British Library Cataloguing in Publication Data. A CIP record for this book can be obtained from the British Library.

All rights reserved. No part of this publication may be reproduced, stored in a retrieval system, or transmitted in any form or by any means, electronic, mechanical, photocopying, recording or otherwise without the prior written permission of the publishers. This book may not be lent, hired out, resold or otherwise disposed of by way of trade in any form of binding or cover other than that in which it is published, without the prior consent of the publishers.

This is a work of fiction. Names, characters, places, events and incidents are either drawn from the author's imagination or used fictitiously. Any resemblance to actual persons, living or dead, or to actual events is coincidental except when citing historical incidents.

Book design by Adam Craig. Cover image © Adam Craig.

Printed in Poland.

Cinnamon Press is represented in the UK by Inpress Ltd www.inpressbooks.co.uk and in Wales by the Welsh Books Council www.cllc.org.uk

The publisher gratefully acknowledges the support of the Welsh Books Council.

I am grateful to the many people who have inspired or assisted the journey of this story. Particular thanks to L, who first introduced me to Saint Casilda; my family for their continual support; the writing groups who have attended courses I've taught and listened to early drafts; Adam Craig for his valuable feedback and for making the research in Spain possible; our hosts in Zaragoza, Burgos and Toledo and Anne Clarke for thoughtful editing suggestions and meticulous copy editing.

To Casilda, for becoming a different story.
To Tamsyn & Finn, who know the power of love and hope.
And to Adam, always.

When life itself seems lunatic, who knows where madness lies? Perhaps to be too practical is madness. To surrender dreams — this may be madness. ... — and maddest of all: to see life as it is, and not as it should be.

...

For hope is always born at the same time as love.

Miguel de Cervantes, *Don Quixote*

Part I

Softly

October 5 2017

In the pre-dawn darkness, Casilda watches the woman approach, pale skin, fair hair spilling around her face, a smile that suggests she is lost in thought. Watching the woman, Casilda feels a jolt, energy deep in her gut. The woman walks past Taberna El Botero, past her, towards the cathedral.

Casilda, she whispers, not knowing why she is saying her name aloud to a passing stranger. I'm your Ben Haddaj, the line runs in her head. I will save you at last, my enchanted girl.

Walking past the cathedral in a loose white dress flecked with embroidery, palest blue like the halo around the sun, the woman reminds her of the girls who come each year for confirmation at Corpus Christi, the whole city decked in flowers. This woman is not much taller, just as slight. She moves further away, turns a corner towards the Museo De La España Mágica. Casilda turns away to continue towards the Sinagoga de Santa Maria Blanca.

Her steps are slower, muscles quiver as she breathes, but the air continues to warm and the street looks the same: the swordmakers on the corner, the window full of damascene. She shakes herself, continues on her path.

This is the beginning and end of the story, she says to herself, turning into the Synagogue.

I was born into a myth of Moorish Iberia, a fragmentary story of a Muslim princess who became a saint and her unrequited lover who disappeared from history and legend while returning to the faith of his Jewish ancestors.

Saint Casilda died a thousand years ago. In some of the stories she was over a hundred years old, in others she was still young. She was cured of an unnatural flow of blood, but perhaps only for a little time.

Twenty-three years ago, my mother, who might have been Casilda in another life, gave birth to me in a flow of blood
—

In the Synagogue, Casilda Faertes sets up instruments in the central aisle. There are no tourists yet and the space is cool, the rows of piers and arcades throw faint shadows and the pinecone details around the horseshoe arches look real. She gazes up, towards the central clam-shell-topped arch, the walls whiter than white, and closes her eyes against the sudden stab of pain in her left temple, rubs away the scent of oranges, notices that behind the pungency there is the faintest tang of roses.

She watches the woman's blood circle down the shower drain, tang of iron on the tongue. It's a cold night, she says to her, the same woman she passed earlier near the taberna, who steps onto the cool cobalt tiles of the tiny bathroom, wet, shaking, but no longer bleeding. She wraps the thin body in a white towel, covers the towel with a white woollen shawl.

Get under the blankets. I'll make you some mint tea.

The woman removes a little hand of Miriam that hangs on a silk cord around her neck and places it on the bedside table of dark wood inlaid with mother of pearl before lying down.

She watches the woman drift into sleep, mint tea cooling on the table.

Casilda?

Casilda shakes herself, blinks into Miguel's face. He stands over her, frowning.

Are you okay?

She shakes herself. Sorry, yes, I'm fine. I thought for a moment I had a migraine looming, but it's lifted.

She has an image of the woman she saw this morning. Did she see her or imagine her? Hardly anyone is on the street at 6.30 in the morning, in October, before sunrise. She can still smell roses, far off, but sweet.

Miguel smiles. I love performing here, he says.

Me too. Not that Quereb's made any progress with Braulio Rodríguez Plaza.

Too much money involved, Miguel says, nodding. Plaza isn't going to give a Synagogue back to Jews when it's such an earner as a museum for the Catholic Church.

They can keep the money. Having the name back would be a gesture in the right direction.

Ibn Shushan Synagogue, formerly known as Santa Maria la Blanca.

Yes. I suppose at least we've got the festival. Half a millennium went by without any being celebrated here.

Hmm, Sukkot in Toledo, a natty little two day affair to replace a religious festival of a week, largely concentrating on food and drink to bring in the tourists. We're just colluding with the spectacle, aren't we? Quaint music to accompany voyeurs gawping at a culture relegated to a relic.

You sound like my mother, Casilda says. I play music because I love it. I sing because I have to. And if the audience think I'm a quaint little zoo-piece, that's their loss. I'm keeping something alive and moving tradition into the present.

Touché and well put, Miguel says, grinning.

Speaking of playing music, what time are the others arriving?

Miguel glances at his watch. Zach should be here soon. Bechor won't be out of bed yet. Wind instruments take all the pneuma out of you, you know, especially when there are women wanting to check out how versatile those lips are.

Casilda laughs. Fair point. Well, Zach can try out the acoustics. I'm in awe of his playing. But Bechor better not be too late, we only have until opening time.

Mm, he's really something, Miguel agrees. And having a finger-picking wonder playing with us can't do any harm, eh? Zach makes me want to visit New York.

Did I hear my name? Zach enters with an entourage of assistants carrying an array of cases. Laouto, cittern, archilaud, viol, guitar, he intones, as though reciting a litany. No Bechor yet? I thought I was late. He turns around, taking in the building. Gotta, love this place, he says.

Yes, Casilda agrees. Mudéjar architecture. Built under Castilian Christians by Islamic architects for a Jewish congregation. How often is that going to happen? And you are late, she adds, smiling, but you still beat Bechor to it. This is his idea of torture, being up before the sun.

Not true, Bechor argues, arms full of slim cases concealing wooden flute, clarinet, kaval and bansuri.

Miguel helps Bechor deposit the instruments safely and they shake hands, throw arms around one another, each slapping the other's back before Bechor turns to do the same to Zach.

Enough with the camaraderie, Casilda quips. Let's rehearse.

Love this nyckelharpa, Zach comments as they arrange themselves. Baltic, isn't it?

It is. My mother had a lover who played one. A Swedish musician and writer. He taught me while he was living with us.

You're still in touch?

Yes. So is my mother, though as friends now. He's an extraordinary artist.

And while I'm asking nosy questions, I keep wondering about your name... it's not...

Jewish? No. Santa Casilda of Toledo. The Muslim princess of this city. She travelled north to a holy well to be cured of a continual flow of blood as a young woman, an adolescent probably. And converted to Christianity.

Your mother is Christian?

No, Jewish, but not Spanish. She was born in Hungary, but grew up in Nice. My mother was fascinated by the story of Santa Casilda. She heard it when she first came to Spain in the '70s. Casilda's the patron of Toledo and my mother lived here for a while. The story stuck with her and she ran into it again later. Santa Casilda died in a sanctuary outside Briviesca, near where my mother settled in Burgos.

And your father? Faertes doesn't sound Hungarian.

I never met him, but he gave me the surname, or rather my mother thought it would be easier for me to have a Spanish surname. Apparently he was from one of those families forcibly converted to Catholicism so long ago that they'd forgotten they ever were Sephardim until it became more popular to dig for our ancestors. So that's me.

Zach nods. Quite right, enough digging. Let's play.

Softly, Casilda says, three hours later. We need to go out softly.

Miguel and Bechor nod.

Just the voice, maybe, Zach adds. At the end, the last notes they hear should be just your voice.

Yes, Miguel agrees. That would be exactly the tone.

Okay, let's do the last verse, just that. Percussion should fade out first, Miguel, then nyckelharpa and cittern. Bechor, keep the bansuri going till the end of the verse, then I'll reprise the last two lines, just voice, very softly. Yes?

Across the city, a young woman in a white dress, embroidered with palest blue says, Softly.

Pardon? The man who looks up is fifteen years her senior, thin and with a face that smiles easily.

Did I say that out loud, Mateo? She laughs. Must be ready for breakfast or perhaps it's brunch now, and getting light-headed. I was remembering a song my mother liked. Simon used to play it.

Your father?

She nods.

I could take you to get something to eat. A thank you for coming in on your day off, and so early. You could tell me more.

That's kind, but I promised to meet a friend. I've been helping her edit her dissertation. She is not sure why she feels the need to lie to Mateo.

He nods in his turn.

She stands and begins to head for the narrow door to the museum, but turns back. Do you ever get the feeling you're being watched?

Watched? Mateo frowns.

Not like a paranoid feeling. More… that someone has seen you, really seen into you, just for a moment. That someone has taken you in and not found you wanting…

Sounds like love, Mateo says wistfully. I see you, if that's what you mean.

Oh. I mean… I… it was on the street early this morning… just fleeting… an odd feeling for hardly a moment…

Ah. I'm not sure I've felt that, but…

I'd better…

Yes, Mateo says. Yes. Have a good brunch with your friend.

Miriam Virág

My darling Casilda,

Some of this you will know, some may be new, but I've often wanted to set it all down for you and now seems to be the right moment. I come from a line of long-lived women. Grand-maman was eighty-eight when she died, her sister, my great-aunt Hélène, eight-three and her daughter, my mother's cousin, Judith, lived to be eighty-nine. But I will be the exception. I am not complaining. My first death certificate was written when I was four years old and here I am, sixty-three, with a good life to look back on. By the time you read this, I won't be here to answer your questions, but I hope this diary will fill in some gaps.

I came to Spain the year Picasso died. Batista and Casals died the same year and, in December, ETA killed Blanco with a bomb in Madrid. The establishment kept its own hands bloodied the following spring, garrotting Salvador Puig. What was I thinking running away to a strange country racked with violence and upheaval? Not about politics. Not then.

All I wanted was to put distance between myself and Grand-maman. We'd been quarrelling for as long as I could remember but, for all my railing against her archaic rules and snobbery, I loved her. And admired her, hugging her story close, telling myself how brave she was.

She left Budapest with nothing. No possessions. No daughter. Only me, a scrawny four year old recovering from scarlet fever. On the journey she told me everything would be new in Paris, even my name. I was no longer Miriam, but Hélène Spire. She showed me a piece of paper I couldn't read, though I'd just learnt to write 'Miriam' in a shaky hand. When I cried, she told me I could still pretend to be Miriam.

We travelled by train to Paris and walked across the city, Grand-maman carrying our tiny shared bag and often carrying me as well.

In Paris we have a home, she told me over and over on the journey. We have a beautiful gallery on a steep street near Sacré Coeur, a white church that looks like a story-book cake. In Paris you'll learn to dance, just like your maman when she was a little girl.

In Paris, we trudged for hours until we stood outside a gallery on a steep street and Grand-maman wept. She wept quietly, but her body shook, filling me with terror. And then she straightened her back and said, No, there is no going back. And we turned and plodded away.

I can't remember how we finally found our way to Nice. It was 1960 and Grand-maman seemed impossibly old, but she was only fifty-seven and soon found a job in a prestigious art gallery on Rue Droite. We had a small apartment on a narrow street, Rue Colonna d'Istria, and I learnt to dance and paint, learnt to love stories, to speak German and French as well as Hungarian and to entertain the stream of visitors to the gallery on Rue Droite. Later, Grand-maman had her own small gallery, further along Rue Droite, on the corner of Rue de la Loge: Atelier Galerie Selene.

I admired how successful she was, how graceful and at ease with the artists. But in private she was always sad. And why shouldn't she be? My grandfather had died in the forced labour service and she and my mother barely made it through the War, starving and sick in a ghetto in Budapest. And then my mother, a single parent, took part in the 1956 uprising and was arrested. I have no memory of my mother and she told no-one who my father was. All she left behind was a scrap of a poem by Attila József and a tiny damascene hamsa. It belonged first to Grand-maman, a gift on her twenty-first birthday during a family trip to Toledo in 1924. She gave it to my mother on her eighteenth birthday.

The hamsa was already old before it was bought for Grand-maman in Toledo. When I was small she would tell me its story and leave it by my bed at night. She had a way of intoning the words that, when I was four or five I scarcely understood, but was comforted by nonetheless. A bedtime litany, though we were not a religious household.

The man who sold it to my mother in Toledo told her that the symbol had been used for hundreds of years, thousands even, Grand-maman always began. This one, he said, is the most rare in my collection, so old I cannot date it, perhaps it has been passed from hand to hand for a thousand years. It is such fine work.

Damascene was practised by the ancient Egyptians, Greeks and Romans, but it was the Syrians of Damascus who perfected it, long before the birth of Christ. The Moors brought it here, to Toledo, and later the Japanese adopted it from Damascus via the Silk Road.

There are forerunners back in the mists of myth: in ancient Mesopotamia it was used to keep the wearer safe. There are Mesopotamian amulets of the open right hand in museums. They called it Qāt Ištar or Inana. It was especially potent for women. And in ancient Egypt they wore a hand with only two fingers and a thumb, the hand of Mano Pantea, the All-goddess, it could represent Isis and Osiris and their child, Horus. There were hamsas in Carthage, dedicated to the supreme goddess, Tanit, used to ward off the evil eye.

The Berbers and Moors brought it here: the hand of Fatima, daughter of Muhammad, a powerful symbol of blessing and protection. And soon it became the hand of Miriam, borrowed from Islam by the Sephardic and Mizrahi Jews, each of the fingers representing the five senses with which to praise God. It appears in Kabbalah as the letter *shin*, the first letter of *Shaddai*, a name of God.

The technique is skilful and difficult. Gold and silver threads are embedded into metal such as black steel, piece by piece. This one, as I said, is the rarest and most intricate hamsa I've ever found. I'll be sorry to see it go. I've refused to sell it more than once, but I feel in my bones it is ready to go with you, the jeweller told my mother.

And so it came to me when I was twenty-one and I gave it to my darling Selene when she was eighteen. And one day it will be yours.

But I left before there was any chance of gift-giving. I left as soon as she told me.

Now that my own daughter is a young woman and I'm older than Grand-maman was when she left Hungary, I have more sympathy for what she did, but then...

She told me how the doctor who'd seen me while I was sick with scarlet fever had a son who worked for the prison services. He suggested that he could help us get out of the country. Grand-maman could take me to Paris, give me a proper home in her own country. He convinced her that, as a foreign national, she would be allowed to leave, but it would be impossible to travel with a Hungarian child. He had the solution; he could get new papers for me as long as I had officially been wiped from the records. Only then, he said, could he arrange for a new identity.

So Grand-maman went along with a terrible plan to tell my mother that I had died of scarlet fever so that the doctor would issue a fake death certificate and we could escape. Of course, he didn't tell Grand-maman what would happen to my mother, that her death sentence would no longer be commuted to life imprisonment if she was not the mother of a living child. Instead, he told her that his son, the prison guard, would let my mother know that we were safe, that he was sure there would soon be pardons and my mother would be able to join us in the not too distant future.

And Grand-maman wrote the letter to Maman informing her that I was dead.

It was my mother's death sentence.

I came to Spain the year I found out that my grandmother had, however unwittingly, killed my mother.

Does Your Mother Know?

October 8 2017

July 16, 1977

We climbed to Draco's rock today. It reminded me of the last time we intended to visit before dawn. If we saw the sun rise over the peak then the slab would move aside for us and we would enter the hidden caves inside the hill.

Of course, Miriam had an episode before we even reached Kirkleatham; the unnatural absence creeping across her face as the fit took her into unconsciousness. I ran to the little row of cottages behind the church and beat on the first door until someone came.

Miriam's mother was incandescent.

Today we made it to the rock without incident, so no wrath from Miriam's mother. Miriam recited the story of Casilda of Toledo as we walked. She was convinced that she saw a Moorish scout about to abduct me in every passer-by and cried at the idea that some boy at school might ask me out. But the worst moment was when she kissed me then said, My mother knows everything.

And yet you named me after her, Miriam says aloud to the empty room, putting down her mother's journal. But I'm not like her, am I? She shakes herself and wanders towards the kitchenette of her tiny apartment, begins pressing coffee grounds into the stove-top pot. And I'm not like Simon either, she says, shivering.

She turns the heat up full, listening for the hiss of scalding coffee percolating into the well. She cradles the turquoise espresso cup in one hand as she sits down at the table that serves also as her desk, flicks through another of her mother's beautifully bound journals piled in front of her.

September 3, 1975

Two days back at school and it's not going well. I keep telling Miriam not to go looking for trouble, to find another way, but I know she won't listen. She led the class assembly today and told them all about Casilda, who lived in the Alcázar of Toledo, a mirror-image of the mother she had never known... right down to details of the 'unnatural flow of blood'. Penny Dean was gobsmacked and Miss Baker hadn't a clue how to handle Miriam.

Gobsmacked, Miriam rolls the word around her mouth, wondering again about the mother she has never known, the mother everyone tells her she is the mirror-image of. She has read the story of Casilda many times, carries one of her mother's copies of *Casilda of the Rising Moon* with her, the hardback edition with its purple cover and line drawing of a girl so like her mother, so like herself, though, like Catherine, Miriam's eyes are grey and her hair fair, not golden.

June 10, 1978

Mandy and Sean's wedding was even more awful than I'd expected. Miriam refused to come with me on the grounds that 'all that disco music' would give her an episode. She was probably right, I could have had a fit (the banned pejorative word) myself — awful music, a family of maudlin drunks and a mock satin bridesmaid dress in a fetching shade of beetroot.

To make it extra-specially dire, Liam came on to me, which reminded me of when The Gang stayed over at the Friends' House in Osmotherley and he tried to put his arm round me. And then Sean cornered me, totally pie-eyed and crying because he didn't think he was good enough for Mandy and how disappointed she would be if he didn't pass his accountancy exams and then, out of nowhere, told me he was with the wrong sister. Too much!

And Miriam hasn't answered the phone all day.

Miriam flicks forward to August '78, her mother's birthday—

I have no idea what possessed Sean to make up such a mad story. What on earth made him tell Mandy we had sex at their wedding? In his dreams! And then to turn up at The House, drunk, brandishing a birthday present and throwing up all over Alex. I hid in Alex and Zoë's attic amongst Zoë's beads, dozed under one of her crocheted shawls, crept down to the landing when I woke and overheard Lorraine filling Miriam's head with poison.

Oh, you're so kind, Miri, but she's still one of *them*, no matter how many books she reads. I mean, fancy screwing her sister's husband on their wedding day. What a cliché. You can't get much lower than that. She's just not what she seems, Little Miss Innocent's just another McManus slut when you scratch the surface.

And then Miriam said, Yes.

I could hardly breathe, steadied myself against the wall, slid down.

Yes, Miriam said again.

How one word can be so small, so brutal. I couldn't keep the story and the facts together... Once there was a Moorish princess, Casilda, daughter of the king of Toledo and a Berber girl, who died in childbirth, I told myself. She had long golden hair, green eyes, pale skin. She wore only white or the palest blue, almost white like the halo of sky around the sun. My hair is fair, not golden, my eyes are grey, but these are only signs of enchantment, I told myself, repeating what Miriam had always insisted.

For six years I have seen only the story that Miriam has told me. Belief was my gift.

But this was the end of the story. I couldn't go on.

And then Liam was there, kneeling on the step below, wrapping himself around me. He's grown tall, over a foot taller than me, broad, brown eyes rich with light, dark hair that frames his face in loose curls. You're okay, Cassie, you're okay, he kept saying, like the start of another story.

Miriam closes the journal. She knows what comes next, Catherine's first marriage to Liam, the miscarriage and divorce, meeting Simon and their time in Budapest, another miscarriage before...

I was born into a myth of Moorish Iberia, a fragmentary story of a Muslim princess who became a saint and her unrequited lover who disappeared from history and legend while returning to the faith of his Jewish ancestors.

Saint Casilda died a thousand years ago. In some of the stories she was over a hundred years old, in others she was still young. She was cured of an unnatural flow of blood, but perhaps only for a little time.

Twenty-three years ago, my mother, who might have been Casilda in another life, gave birth to me in a flow of blood—

That was nearly-perfect, Casilda says, grinning at Zach, Bechor and Miguel. God, I hope we play like that tonight when we've got an audience.

We'll be even better, Zach says, beginning to pick a melody idly on his guitar. More adrenalin, more buzz. Don't know about you guys, but a crowd raises my game.

Awesome, Bechor says in a mock-American accent that doesn't quite mimic Zach's Manhattan clip.

I'm sure I know that tune, but I can't place it, Casilda tells Zach, head on one side, listening.

Canadian folk singer...

Gordon Lightfoot, Casilda completes.

You really do know a wide range of music, don't you? 'Does Your Mother Know'... Zach begins to sing quietly.

Casilda laughs. My mother knows everything. And, as you might expect, I know Gordon Lightfoot from another one of her lovers.

Across the city, Miriam's mobile vibrates against the table and an image of Eliška appears on the screen.

Darling, you sound tired.

Miriam laughs. I am. I've been working on a tough translation, and then drifted into reading Catherine's journals. I haven't eaten yet.

Go out to eat.

I can't, I'm a student. I have to live frugally.

Nonsense, I'll send you money for your birthday. Anyway, doesn't that job pay you? Go to that delightful taberna and get tapas.

El Botero? It feels a bit sad going there alone, unless it's a for morning coffee with my notebook. And my birthday's over three weeks away. You can't keep sending me gifts.

Of course I can, but even better, call that guy that's keen on you, the one…

Mateo? I can't. I mean, I work with him.

But you like him?

He's… Miriam hesitates. If I wrote myself an ideal partner he'd be it, well maybe not the fifteen years older part. I don't want to be one of those women trying to replace her father, but otherwise… it's just…

Just what?

There's something missing, something… she trails away.

Don't be too picky, Miriam. You can waste your life while you're waiting for *the one*. Nathan was a disaster, but we had a lot of fun for a while. I'd still do it again.

But you've had no-one since, Miriam reminds her. And you broke up when I was barely thirteen.

I was married to my work and he to his and he went even further into himself after Simon... Anyway, I was happy looking after you.

And now?

Now I'm in my fifties and too used to my own company. But we're not talking about me—whatever you decide to do this evening, don't spend it buried in your mother's journals.

It's the only way I can know her, Miriam says softly.

I know, darling, I know, but I hate thinking of you alone and brooding.

I'm fine, Miriam reassures. And I'll eat, I promise. She pauses. Did she know, do you think? I mean did she know she was going to...

She hears Eliška's breath catch. I don't think so, darling, but I've told you this before. And, of course, I wasn't there. Simon would only say...

I'm sorry. I know I keep repeating the question, but I still wonder. I wonder if she was afraid or if she thought... Do you think she thought she'd live again, in another body, still working out this one amazing relationship across history?

Simon said all she thought about was you.

And sometimes all I think about is her. I ache for her, especially when I'm here. Maybe she really was Casilda and maybe...

Miriam?

Sorry. I just remembered the oddest moment from a few days ago—a woman passed me on the the street, about my age, beautiful, with long dark hair, and I thought I heard her call me, but she called me Casilda and then…

Yes?

In my mind I heard, I'm your Ben Haddaj…

And so it goes, Eliška says quietly. For hope is always born…

That's what my mother…

Yes. For hope is always born at the same time as love. The last thing Catherine said.

Miriam Virág

Growing up in Nice in the '60s and early '70s, I learnt how to dance and paint, sing and tell stories, how to converse in several languages and, of course, how to make love.

We were in the midst of the Trente Glorieuses, first with de Gaulle's politique de grandeur and later with Pompidou's dirigisme, state-directed capitalism to expand the economy.

A few years later, when Picasso took a house in Mougins, Grand-maman decided we must move there too, leaving behind the small apartment on Rue Colonna d'Istria for a hilltop village, but it was one of the rare arguments I won with her. I wanted to stay by the sea, to continue learning with my beloved dance teacher and I did not want to be the outsider again, not at the grand age of almost ten. And so we stayed in Matisse's town, but moved to a larger apartment where we could continue to entertain the visitors to Grand-maman's newly acquired gallery two floors beneath us. Grand-maman always maintained she had never really thought of leaving, that it was just a passing notion. Money follows art, was a favourite saying of hers and, by the time Chagall began work on the Musée national message biblique Marc Chagall, she had convinced herself that not even for one moment had she ever imagined leaving Nice.

In my last year there, the Chagall museum became my favourite place. I could lose myself in those huge canvasses of stories from *Genesis* and *Exodus*, and most especially in the *Song of Solomon* canvases.

After running away from Nice so abruptly, I returned only once. It was July 1991 and Grand-maman had died, aged eighty-eight. I'd kept a distant watch through a friend from my dancing school days and she had never betrayed me. I didn't attend the funeral. By the time Nathalie let me know, the funeral was only a day away. My lover, Esben, insisted I could leave you with him. But you were only a little over seven months and I was still breastfeeding. I didn't think I could face Grand-maman's graveside alone and worrying about her, so I travelled with you, my baby daughter, to make my peace. But I felt none.

I had dinner with Nathalie the evening I arrived and she told me that Grand-maman had left everything to me in her will. She handed me a card with the lawyer's address and the next day I made an appointment and sat in his office, you on my knee gurgling happily, feeling stupefied as he told me how much Atelier Galerie Selene and Grand-maman's apartment were worth.

Of course, there are also a considerable number of art works, he added. Your grandmother had built an extraordinary personal collection over many years, as I'm sure you know. It will take time to value, but if you wish to sell the pieces...

No, I told him. No, I couldn't sell them.

Something in me screamed to walk away, to take nothing,

but I had you to think of and I knew many of those artworks from growing up with Grand-maman. I told him I needed time to process all of this. I wandered back to Nathalie's apartment, dazed, and she wrested you from me and told me to walk and think.

I wandered to the Chagall museum without thinking where I was going. I sat in front of 'Moses with the Burning Bush', and felt myself falling:

... numinous burning, red and yellow against blue-blue-blue. Moses on his knees, transfigured—and I am transformed with him—the power of being: I will be who I will be. Raw energy. To be, to be new, to go on being, not to expire—to have a future—burning, always, not consumed. I was. I am. I will be. Will I?

I heard the words in my head, but they were not mine. I brushed away a stray tear and followed a young woman as she too moved on to 'Noah's Ark':

... blue-blue waters rising, a bird here, goat there. And the people, waiting in the wings of apocalypse, huddled. Who will make it? There are mothers holding children, families clustered, a man on his knees, behind him a woman stands, head bent to his, arms wrapping him. Will they make it?

How many can an Ark hold? And the covenant, what is that? The rainbow promise of no more destruction? I was surprised to realise I'd asked the questions out loud and the woman turned to me, a pale woman with grey eyes and long fair hair.

No-one can make that promise, not even God, she said very quietly, replying to my French in English. Sometimes the story and the facts don't match.

I watched her turn away and walk towards the next canvas and in my head:

... blue tribulation. Jacob meets the love of his life at the well and how does that go? Fourteen years before they are together. And his beloved child, his son—all that love come to tears, blood, betrayal, loss. And in the middle of this Jacob meets what? Who? Does he fight the ground of being for a place to stand? Jacob—violet on blue, struggling, fighting, changed—

She didn't look at me when I stood beside her at the next canvas. The Chagall obviously haunted her and her thoughts haunted me:

... so we fight with being itself to discover who we are; limp on, walking out of a past of victories and defeats and into a future of unimagined losses, fears and hopes; wounded and blessed.

In the room of *Le Cantique des Cantiques* the canvasses were red.

The woman started to weep, clutching her stomach.

Madame? An attendant reached out a hand tentatively, but pulled it back as she looked up. *Madame? Vous êtes...*

She shook her head. I'm fine. She brushed a hand ineffectually across her face, smiled weakly. It's just the pictures... they're very moving.

The attendant nodded, moved away, glancing back at her.

I hovered nearby, unsure whether to ask this stranger, whose thoughts I was sure I had overheard, if she was okay, but she spoke first. A slight smile. Catherine, she offered.

Miriam, I replied.

She startled slightly at my name and I noticed she was wearing a hand of Miriam, a hamsa that appeared identical to the one Grand-maman should have given me on my eighteenth birthday.

I had a friend called Miriam, she offered, but she died. This hand of Miriam was a gift from her.

My grandmother had one, I said in return. She died two days ago. I'm here to visit her grave.

Catherine nodded. I used to believe. Before I lost Miriam, lost my baby, but now...

I nodded. I don't think I've ever believed, not in a traditional sense, and yet...

The world is a strange place, she finished for me.

It is.

We fell silent, then said goodbye at the same instant, laughed and shook hands, though I wanted to hug her, to hold onto her. She left and I had a feeling of such loss that finally the tears for Grand-maman came.

Go My Way

April 2018

She is not sure why she has finally said yes to Mateo. She remembers confiding too much to him one day as they were closing up after a busy Saturday at the Museum. It must have been around the time of El Dia de los Muertos. She had become maudlin, thinking of the mother she'd never known, thinking about Simon. She might even have cried, not wept, but allowed a stray tear to escape. He'd reached a hand around her shoulder. You know you're beautiful, he'd whispered. He'd asked her for a drink, they could go somewhere afterwards to get food, talk more.

Thinking of the dead should be done in company, he said.

She was so tired and had been staying up late to work on her dissertation, feeling herself circling the crux of what she wanted to say and feeling the elusiveness of her protagonist in the accompanying novella that had to be good enough to submit for her MA, and sleeping badly, and dreaming about that day on the beach… and missing Eliška and…

Yes, she said.

Really? Mateo almost startled. That's great, he said, recovering, smiling.

I should go home first and change.

You're beautiful as you are, he told her, but he seemed to be following her thoughts and added, How about a drink first at El Botero, then we can nip back to your place and you can change for dinner if you like?

Okay.

She drank a Raspberry Sidecar, invented by the flamboyant, talented bartender, who always wore dicky bows and sleeves held back with garters above his tattoos. Then followed it with the barman's own version of an Old Fashioned on a stomach empty since breakfast and felt her balance was off as she and Mateo walked the short distance back to her little apartment. Inside, she opened windows and poured water for them both, settled Mateo with an extract of her novella and a CD of Erik Satie.

Just a quick shower and I'll be ready.

No rush. Mateo looked up from the print-out. This is good.

At dinner she'd told him more about Simon and Eliška and their fascination with mediaeval occultism, about Catherine's obsession with Casilda of Toledo and the novels and journals she'd left behind. They shared a bottle of Cencibel wine from Finca Loranque and, later, he walked her home, not commenting when she leaned on him for balance, not objecting when she'd told him she felt a bit odd and thought she should go straight to bed, to sleep. He made mint tea and left a tiny cobalt bowl of it by her bed, pulled a white wool shawl over her and closed the door quietly as he left.

He's a good man, she thinks, glancing in the mirror, then checking her bag for keys and purse before she leaves. He's a good man and in a few months I'll leave Toledo and he'll feel betrayed.

She walks uphill on Calle Pozo Amargo from her apartment at Cuesta de los Escalones, 5, a tiny stepped passage of buildings, and turns right on Calle Ciudad. It's less than ten minutes walk to the El Tránsito synagogue, the extraordinary 14th century Mudéjar building with its profusion of geometric and floral motifs, inscriptions in Arabic and Hebrew and the elegant, three-storey parquet-floored main chamber where the concert of Sephardi music is being performed.

Mateo is waiting outside when she arrives, looking stylish in chinos and a suede jacket.

I'm so glad we saw the leaflet, Miriam says, hugging him. I was really disappointed when I realised I'd missed them last October.

The poster on the door shows the silhouette of a woman, back to the viewer, walking across a blue field towards a startling harvest moon: leyendas de la luna, the title runs. At the bottom, a headshot of each of the musicians, their names in small clear letters: Casilda Faertes with Zach Buchmann, Bechor Abeidano and Miguel Zapatero.

Not what you'd think of as a Sephardi name, Mateo comments. But she certainly looks the part.

Miriam peers at the young woman, wild dark hair around an oval face. I'm sure I've seen her before, she says.

Probably on posters, Mateo says, taking her hand and leading her inside.

Miriam shivers as the singer begins. It's her, she says.

Mateo glances at her quizzically.

It's the woman who called me Casilda, Miriam whispers.

He knits his brows, but says nothing.

And Miriam loses herself, the music taking her...

A shadow pale as dust flits across a mote of light, the fragrance of roses suffusing the air. Somewhere a string is plucked, faint music —

> *Al-'ūdu qud tarannam*
> *Bi-abdā'i talhîn*
> *Wa ṣaqqod al-madā nib*
> *Riyād al-basātîn*

...a sound of water against stone. Is there a word in the breeze? *Tulaytula.*

Remember, my darling Casilda. Remember... and if you can't remember, invent...

Remember how you heard the story of Saint Marina, were fascinated by a king's daughter who ran away to lead a contemplative's life...

...there is a rustle of silk, shadows beneath vaulted arches... water bells against stone, whispers, *Casilda.*

She feels Mateo gently nudge her and... The music has stopped and Casilda Faertes is addressing the audience. She thanks them for listening, for being so appreciative, continues:

It's always a delight to return to Toledo, where I studied at the conservatory and learned to busk on the streets. Toledo is a city rich in heritage and beauty, a place that has seen cultures mix and influence each other in the best way. It's a place that inspires me and I love getting lost here. It's a place full of history, spirituality and culture and we need that more than ever. Sadly, the bookings we get are too often only to fulfil tourist curiosity...

Miriam notices one of the young musicians, Miguel, she thinks, reach a hand out to Casilda as though to warn her to stop. But Casilda moves away slightly and the American musician says quietly into his microphone, You go, girl.

Music is not thought of as real work or culturally valuable in Spain. What little support there is for concerts or imaginative projects is marginalised and often relies on who you know. We are a corrupt country. Most people don't see how vital music is to life and we don't even have a union of musicians. We live in a time where culture and vision hardly survive. At times I feel as though all I can do is leave, but then I return to Toledo and I'm reminded that we have so much heritage, even if sometimes we have apparently wanted to destroy it and... Well, all I really wanted to say...

There is a ripple of nervous laughter amongst the audience. Is she going to say something about anti-Semitism, about the situation in Catalonia...

All I really wanted to say is that you have been a wonderful audience who I know take seriously the contribution of music and appreciate what it is for cultures to work together. Thank you.

There is loud applause. People begin to stand, clapping vigorously, calling for another melody and Casilda smiles and nods, picks up her nyckelharpa and bow, her clear, haunting voice filling the space as the musicians behind her weave melodies into the magic.

Later, Miriam queues, clutching the CD to be signed, Mateo standing beside her patiently.

Casilda startles slightly as Miriam hands her the disc. You're...

We met... well not exactly met, but... I thought you called me Casilda...

Last October, Casilda says. You were wearing a white dress with blue embroidery.

Miriam nods and beside her Mateo shifts uneasily. His smile is tense. Sorry, dinner reservations... we...

Have we? Miriam asks.

Well if you don't have reservations, you must join us, Casilda says. We're going to La Abadia. Do you know it?

Oh, no... I'm afraid we... Mateo begins.

I know where it is, Miriam cuts in. Round the corner from Cristo de la Luz? I've never eaten there, but...

I'm afraid we do have reservations, Mateo insists.

Well, another time then, Casilda says, I'm afraid I should sign these... she gestures to the waiting queue. But if you can make it...

Thank you, Mateo says, taking Miriam's arm, leading her towards the exit.

But... She looks back. At the door she says to Mateo, I think I'm getting a migraine. I'm sorry. I think I need to get home.

Not to La Abadia?

Miriam frowns. I'm a free agent, Mateo. She rubs her temple. I'm sorry. I don't mean to snap. Do you smell oranges?

Oranges?

Yes, really strong. I think I might be sick.

He puts an arm around her, but she doesn't relax into him. They walk in silence, bodies stiff, stop at the corner of Calle Pozo Amargo.

I'll be fine from here, Miriam says. No need to go my way. Thank you for an amazing evening, she adds.

I'll see you at work then, Mateo says, his voice flat.

He looks tired and she reaches out a hand and touches his arm. Yes, she says, see you at work.

As she turns into the cobbled street, a heavy clot of blood slip between her legs. Unsteady, she glances round. Mateo has gone. She huddles into her shawl, feels oozing through the thin fabric of her dress, makes her way down the lane, abdomen aching, pain digging above her left eye.

She thinks of Catherine. There was no way to stop the blood, Simon had told her once.

She pushes against the heavy wooden door, limps across the herringboned brick floor of the courtyard and up the worn wooden steps to her door., her hand clammy on the metal rail.

Inside, she stands on the cool cobalt tiles of the bathroom, lets water scald and saturate every sense.

Blood strews the drain crimson, tang of iron on tongue, water sears, soothes.

A shadow pale as dust flits across a mote of light, the fragrance of roses suffusing the air. Somewhere a string is plucked, faint music—

> *Al-'ūdu qud tarannam*
> *Bi-abdā'i talhīn*
> *Wa saqqod al-madā nib*
> *Riyād al-basātîn*

When she steps out of the shower, the blood has eased to a trickle. She slides between white cotton sheets, falls into deep sleep clutching the hand of Miriam that she wears always.

Miriam Virág

It took me many years to find this home in Burgos.

Spanish was not one of my languages, though I'd heard it spoken sometimes in Nice and I soon picked up enough to get work in bars or tabernas. I was working in a café in Madrid when a bomb, thought to have been planted by ETA, killed twelve people and injured more than seventy others in Café Rolando. It wasn't close to the café I worked in, but it scared me anyway and I was already hankering for somewhere smaller than Madrid. I gave in my notice the next day.

What was it that Quixote said? *The unreason of the world is more insane than any fiction.* It was true in Cervantes' time and true in his homeland in the '70s. Within a year, Gonzalez was rallying the Socialist Workers' Party, Spain had withdrawn from the Spanish Sahara and Juan Carlos had taken over power at Franco's insistence. Franco died in November and the Cervantes' Prize for Literature was founded, a double victory for the man who'd tilted at windmills even when he was sure to lose.

I spent that winter in Toledo. It was a cold year, sometimes as low as 3°. I got work in a taberna, but they didn't need me for many hours so I put up a notice in the local grocer advertising dance lessons for children and soon had a group of small girls to teach in a room at the back of the restaurant. Between these two trickles of income, I eked out a meagre and happy existence in a place that fascinated me. Toledo resonated to a Moorish past — the tiles on the walls, the dishes in the tabernas, the curved swords displayed in shops, the keyhole archways, the Arabic designs on the intricate damascene jewellery of oxidised black steel inlaid with filigree silver and gold, that adorned every other shop window.

I imagined my Grand-maman visiting here for her twenty-first birthday in 1924. It was hard to picture her as a vivacious young woman. She'd been given the damascene hand of Miriam that had come from one of the shops I passed each day. The hamsa whose story I'd heard again and again.

In the tenth century cave that houses the Museo De La España Mágica, I felt that I had stepped into another time. On the walls of the entrance, two hands of Fatima, one of them perfectly preserved, surrounded by three elegant dark birds of paradise.

The hand of Miriam, I said out loud, beginning to cry for the hamsa that Grand-maman had given my mother when I was born, that would have been given to me on my eighteenth birthday if I hadn't left so abruptly. I glanced around, feeling self-conscious, relieved that I was the only visitor.

I spent hours in the cool, columned space of what had once been the Ibn Shushan Synagogue, now Santa Maria la Blanca, and whole afternoons in the tiny Cristo de la Luz, dancing alone in the little square end of the building, the part that had once been a mosque, Mezquita Bab al-Mardum. It was deserted in December and my apartment was too small to practice in, so I would circle the four central columns that rose slender and elegant into capitals that took various elements of palm leaves, pirouette under horseshoe arches, move between the nine ceiling vaults, gazing at their intricate designs. Sometimes I would visit when the mosque was closed, slipping over the metal fence at its lowest point and ducking under the bridge to the ticket office before climbing another metal fence at the bottom of the steps to the mosque's courtyard. Though it hadn't been a Muslim place of worship for hundreds of years, I always covered my head in a scarf. There was something sacred yet comforting about the place. And, looking up through cusped arches, light reflecting on white stone, I had the oddest sensation that my mother had been here before me, though it couldn't have been the case.

On one cool, bright day, as I was leaving the garden, I thought I heard a rustle like silk on skin, saw the shadow of a slender girl in white, but it was only air thickening in shadows beneath vaulted arches, screened from winter glare by panels of wooden lattice.

In the mosque gardens, trees bowed under approaching winter, dry leaves shimmered as the last of them fell and the large cedar bent to the wind. The fountain by the back wall no longer ran, yet sometimes I would turn towards a sound of water against stone. And once there was a word on the breeze. *Tulaytula.*

I stayed in Toledo until the next autumn, until my lover began to talk about meeting his family, about our future. I slipped away, not knowing where I would go next or what I would do when I got there. I knew only that Agustin was not my future and that a voice was calling me north, telling me: until death, it's all life, Miriam—there's a remedy for all things, except death.

If You Could Read My Mind

June 20 2018

Miriam stands looking at the papers scattered across the table. On top of the pile a form marked, Disertación de Máster Universitario en Investigación en Letras y Humanidades., beneath which she has written: Una investigación sobre la influencia del sufismo en la alquimia midiaeval y la Cábala judía de Geber a Moses de Leon y sus usos en el desarrollo de una novela alquímica del siglo XXI. (An Investigation of the Influence of Sufism on Mediaeval alchemy and Kabbalah from Geber to Moses de Leon and its uses in developing a 21st Century Alchemical Novel.)

She wakes her laptop and glares at the abstract for her dissertation, eradicates a comma, sighs, puts it back, scrolls down the screen, glances over the table of contents:

The role of Jabir Ibn Hayyan (aka Geber) in 8th century Arabic alchemy and
13th Century Latin Alchemical texts by 'Geber' (aka Pseudo-Geber):
    the problem of translation, plagiarism or originality
    in Pseudo-Geber
Mystical Alchemical Investigation:
    Takwin
    Numerology

From Sufism to Kabbalah:
- Dissenting voices:
  - Halkin, Scholem and Dan:
    - Kabbalah as a wholly Jewish concept without Sufi influence

Sufi Influence on Kabbalah
- Sufism in the pre-Kabbalist:
  - Moses, Abraham and Obadyah Maimonides
  - Solomon Ibn Gabirol
  - Judah Halevi

Direct Sufi influences:

Parallels Between Jabir Ibn Hayyan and the *Sefer Yetzirah*
- The Mystical Meanings of Letters: from *Qu'ran Surahs* to the *Sefer Bahir*
- Developing Kabbalah: from mystical calligraphy to the erotic Shekinah
- The Ten Words of Creation:
  - the mystical fruit (Sephiroth) in comparison to the Islamic Tree of Life

The Emergence of the *Zohar*:
- Moses de Leon:
  - 'rediscovering 2nd Century Talmud or Mining Sufi Lore?

Kabbalistic Themes in Fiction:
- From German Romanticism to Hawthorne's 'The Birthmark'
- From Mary Shelley to George Eliot
- Kabbalah in the Contemporary Novel:
  - Case Studies: Lisa Goldstein, Ted Chiang & Helene Wecker

At the confluence of religions:
- re-imagining Casilda through alchemy and Kabbalah in my novella *Crossing Over*.

Appendix 1
- *Crossing Over*: a work in progress.

References

She scrolls through the document rapidly, catching stray words as she goes, stops at a section on takwin, the synthetic creation of life. Growing up in Prague in her teens, the figure of the golem had been everywhere, a tourist token to be carried home as a tiny clay figure in the bottom of a suitcase. But she loved the story of the golem hiding away in the now sealed-off attic of the Old New Synagogue, ready to defend the remnant of the Jewish community that Eliška belonged to, should the need arise again.

In his *Book of Stones* (4:12) Jabir Ibn Hayyan writes that the material on takwin is deliberately confusing so that only those God loves will be able to interpret it. The text is full of baffling symbols with contended interpretations, perhaps because assuming the god-like powers of creation, with all the spiritual transformation implied by such power, creates an uneasy relationship between Islamic science, magic and the more traditional notions of revelation.

She scrolls further, stops at a quote from McGaha:

It was no coincidence that the earliest Kabbalistic writings and the work of (Sufi philosopher) Ibn Arabi appeared around the same time (late 12th-early 13th-centuries). Jewish refugees from Muslim Spain were breathing new life into the doctrines and imagery developed by the Sufis in Baghdad and later in Andalusia, creating the new system of mysticism known as the Kabbalah.

Jewish refugees from Muslim Spain. She has a sudden image of a woman she passed on the street. Not recently, last autumn. Casilda. The woman had called her Casilda and then she was sure she'd heard: *I'm your Ben Haddaj. I'm supposed to save you, my darling girl.* Though by then the woman had walked past. She'd met her again at a concert: Casilda Faertes had invited her and Mateo to La Abadia to eat with the musicians, but...

She flicks down the lid of the computer. I'm not ready, she says to the empty room. And no-one is going to save me.

She should phone Eliška, but she doesn't want to worry her, telling her that she thinks her dissertation is lacking in... she's not even sure what... Or that the beginning of her novella, the reimagining of the story of the saint who had fascinated her once Catholic mother, feels flat and... She shakes herself. She will hand in the dissertation and the novella, whatever the outcome.

She surveys the mess of her mother's journals, diaries in which Catherine had wondered if she might once have been Casilda in another life, others chronicling her time in Budapest, dreaming the life of a woman from the Fifties, imprisoned, the woman remembering a lover who she could not possibly have met, who killed himself decades before her child was born, decades before her life was stripped away by imprisonment in an inhuman system. Were the journals any more than overwrought ramblings? Beside the older journals, three beautifully bound notebooks in purples and greens, the last one written while Catherine was pregnant for the last time, together with an assortment of notes written by Simon and postcards from Eliška.

Miriam balls her fists into her eyes, breathes deeply. She walks to the kitchenette and pours water, wanders into the bedroom and out onto the tiny balcony perched over the flat below, gazes towards the Alcázar.

Music drifts from somewhere below, not the usual Luis Fonsi and Daddy Yankee's *Despacito* on repeat, which seems to be everywhere, but piano music, the elegant legato of Chopin's Nocturne in E-flat major, its opening cadences barely audible...

There is a scent of oranges, the pulse of the music more insistent.

Beneath the balcony, a girl of about sixteen smiles up at her. She has olive skin, hair a tangle of soot and pitch. Miriam thinks she has seen her before... a long time ago in Prague, but... she looks like the woman on the street who called her 'Casilda', a younger version perhaps... yet still the memory of Prague...

I brought your cure when you were weak, almost dead, Casilda, the girl is saying. the talisman that would bring your cure, knowing that you had secretly given your heart to Christian's saviour, risking your father's wrath. I made a vow then that if the relic cured you, if you lived, I would return to the religion of my fathers, to the God of Abraham, Isaac and Jacob. When I arrived in Toledo your father was beyond himself with grief. I had a hard time persuading King Alamun to allow me even one minute alone with you and your nurse. You were so pale that, for a moment, I thought I'd arrived too late, but your eyes flickered and you told me you had been expecting me. I had brought you a scrap of the Virgin's robe, dipped in holy water, and I knew that if you had found faith you would live. You said simply, I believe, and were well again. It wasn't the relic of course. It wasn't magic that healed you, but faith. Belief is your gift. I believe, you said, and then you were laughing and well and Alamun and his men were in the room, swords drawn, amazed to see you sitting up, healthy and happy.

I knew the price of saving you would be terrible. That I would be betrothed to your sister Zoraida as a reward, that I could not refuse the powerful Alamun and his son Ahmed. I was like Abraham commanded to kill his son. I had been commanded to put aside my love for you in order to save you.

The girl drops her voice to a whisper. God always demands a sacrifice, Casilda, even after saying He's through with it.

He's been in her dreams since she was twelve years old. The beach goes on forever… They're chatting about the weather, what he will work on after the holiday when Nathan and Eliška have returned to London.

I don't think they're very happy together, he says, as though confiding to another adult. I wouldn't be surprised if Eliška left him.

She won't go back to Prague?

He puts an arm around her shoulder. We'd miss her, wouldn't we?

Miriam nods.

But we'd stick together, the two of us. There is a movement so small, so strange, something in the way he tucks her into his thin frame…

No, Miriam shouts. No. She pulls away.

Miriam! It's fine… I was… I was just thinking… He reaches out to her. You look like you're reading my mind… but…

She pushes him away again, begins to run.

Eliška, she calls, running towards the cottage. Eliška!

And she's there, coming through the gate, running to meet her. Miriam, what's the matter? Where's your father? Where's Simon?

She begins to sob, clings to her aunt, crying.

He's been in her dreams for twelve years, the dream never reaches the end. The story and the facts don't match.

Miriam rubs her temple, shivers in the warm evening air. There is no music, no girl.

On the table, a card depicting the Fool from the Prague Tarot lies on top of her pile of notes. She turns it over, reads:

28.09.2016.

Darling Miriam,

I hope you are settling in Toledo. It's so quiet here without you and I'm not used to being alone, but I think of you writing and researching where Catherine and Simon left off and am full of pride.

My life jogs along as always. Sometimes, on walks, I watch the poor suckers who work at the Speculum Alchemiae, leading witless tourists around the 'The Magical Triangle'. I'm grateful to be hidden away in the research archive at the Castle, though it's fun to think of others dealing in Prague's alchemical past in their various ways. Speculum Alchemiae is at least a step-up from the hocus at The House of the Donkey in the Cradle, where Edward Kelley certainly did not live. It's a shame they couldn't have put the 'museum' into his Faustus House in Charles Square, at least it would have been grander and that house has provenance. But I suppose it's fitting that a fraudster like Kelley is now immortalised in a building that is pretending to be the home where he swapped wives with Dee and allegedly nurtured Shakespeare.

Well, that was off topic and I'm running out of space. What I meant to write was that I'm proud of you. Hodně štestí, or should I say buena suerte, in your quest for reimagining Casilda.

Much love always,
Eliška.

But two years later, is she any closer to finding Casilda? She has visited all the sites, read the literature, lingered often in Mesquita del Cristo de la Luz, and yet...

In two days time she will head to Burgos. She knows from previous visits that there is no trace of Casilda in the Cathedral. Whatever stood on the site before the florid Gothic colossus with its gold altar pieces and crystal domes has been obliterated, leaving no hint of an older Burgos. But she will visit the castle. It is only two circles of thick walls with traces of towers, a few pillars where the palace stood, yet she can look out from there towards the sanctuary beyond Briviesca, more than forty kilometres along the Camino de los Romanos, the way Casilda must have walked. She can imagine the chapel in the palace, feel that she is standing on the spot where Casilda was baptised a thousand years ago. And then she will travel to Briviesca and say good bye to Casilda's remains before returning to Prague. To do what? She shivers.

Thank you for staying in the world with me, she says, putting Eliška's card back onto the pile.

Miriam Virág

I left Toledo a few days before Spain was declared a democracy. It was one of the rare times I gave much thought to what might be happening in Hungary, the country where I was born, where my mother was executed. Only months after my mother was brutally dispatched, Kádár had swapped tactics, no longer targeting 'revolutionaries', but declaring a new slogan: He who is not against us is with us. There was a general amnesty and constraints put on the secret police.

I thought about Hungary again about a month later, when a Hungarian art forger, Elmyr de Hory, took a barbiturate overdose in Ibiza. Had Grand-maman ever bought one of his fakes, I wondered. After all, his first fake sale was a pen and ink drawing mistaken for a Picasso.

I drifted to Barcelona that winter, but was determined not to take bar work. Instead, I tramped around dance studios until I found one that would let me teach the kindergarten students, a miniature studio in a backstreet off Carner de Sant Fructuós, where tiny girls in candyfloss nylon tutus giggled and pranced together. But soon Estudio Ria Moline was not only giving me more work, but also encouraging me to leave. Ria had learnt to dance at the Real Conservatorio Profesional de Danza Mariemma in Madrid and was determined that I should follow in her footsteps. So in 1977, while Spain slumped under a banking crisis, I returned to Madrid, found the smallest possible room above a tapas bar on Calle de Melilla and divided my time between being a student of the dance school and a tutor at another studio full of giggling or recalcitrant schoolgirls. I lived like a nun for six years, learning dance every morning for four or five hours, then teaching it for three or four hours from the close of school into the evening every weekday and longer on Saturdays.

For six years I closed myself off from the world, from thoughts of family, from any possibility of love, from whatever might be happening around me, taking no notice of the new constitution and its seventeen autonomous regions, of Spain joining NATO or the victory of the Socialist Workers in the 1982 election. I emerged lean, supple, ignorant and hungry to be in the world again.

It was late 1983. I was twenty-eight, owned nothing and had roots nowhere. I set off to Zaragoza, with no more thought than wanting to be in a city with a Moorish past, but not wanting to return to Toledo, where I might run into Agustin. As I travelled, a small voice whispered that Grand-maman must be eighty now and perhaps I should... but I resisted. I sent a postcard to Nathalie and asked only if all was well in Nice. And she replied as ambiguously, but it was enough to know that Grand-maman was well. It was enough then, but now it will never be enough. That chance passed many years ago.

In Zaragoza, a labyrinthine place, I got lost on every trip to the market, swearing that places moved around overnight. It was a city where great artists like Goya and Saura began, but seemed always to leave. Yet the city buzzed with the discoveries being made as the 6,000-seat amphitheatre of the former Roman city of Cesaraugusta was excavated, and the Aljafería Palace drew me back and back to sit under trellised arches listening to water tinkle along irrigation channels into the pool and to beautiful finches celebrating their nests in the plump orange trees, the fruit hanging like ornaments on a Christmas tree.

I set up a studio near the Basílica de Nuestra Señora del Pilar, above a tiny taberna that served cheap tapas and cheaper wine. I tried to imagine it might be like the studio where my mother had learned to dance in the Marais when she was a girl. Zaragoza, though nothing like Paris nor Madrid, was a friendly, cultured place and I welcomed its distinctiveness, the fierce Cierzo that blew in the autumn and winter, and sometimes even in the hot summers, which Cato had once described as *a wind that fills your mouth and tumbles wagons and armed men*; the bitter cold in December and January and the sudden drenching rains in April and May.

From my attic apartment over the studio, I looked out across thirteen domed and minareted towers of the basilica and, a little further away, the galleried tower of La Seo Cathedral, where once a mosque had stood. By day I watched swifts dart over red-tiled roofs against the backdrop of the basilica and, in the evening, I delighted in bats swooping to eat half their body weight in mosquitoes.

I taught. I danced. I went to showings of Buñuel films, popular in the year of his death. He'd come to live in Zaragoza, from the Aragonese town of Calanda, with his rich family at the age of four, and had discovered atheism here. I listened to struggling pop rock bands in smoke-filled bars where people spoke enthusiastically about the music festival from three years before as though it was still happening. I followed Héroes del Silencio to every local gig, jarred by their aggressive hard rock edge, but entranced by the sudden shifts to melancholy and plaintive lyrics and dream-like guitar solos. I visited any art exhibition I could find.

And I met Rafael.

Song for a Winter's Night

August 2018

02.08.2016.

My darling Miriam,

I wish I was there with you. I'm so sorry that you feel no closer to Casilda after your time in Burgos, or rather that you feel as though you are missing something, that there is an answer just out of your field of vision, that you turn and it has gone. Try to be patient with yourself. You have two years to write and think, and perhaps Toledo will speak to you over that time. In fact, I'm sure it will.

I can't answer for your parents, but I know that you were everything Catherine hoped for, that she loved you completely, even if she knew you for only a few minutes. As to what her journals might mean, I can't be sure, but sometimes I feel that you and she are one and the same, working out a story that stretches across time.

As to Simon, I feel the weight of his loss every day. I know he had moments when he looked at you and saw only Catherine and that those moments were becoming more frequent, becoming unbearable. He had always struggled and I think he found himself too confused. In my worst moments I think *what if...* but if I had saved him that day, I think another would have come along... But you must never think that his love for you was not enough to keep him in the world. Rather he wanted his love for you to stay... unclouded... And in his anguish I can only think that he imagined he was protecting you by leaving.

Anyway, my love, don't give up on Burgos entirely. The tomb at Briviesca certainly seems absurd, all that red and gold and the cherubs flying over her. She hardly looks like a poor hermit in repose from the pictures you sent of the gaudy marble sepulchre, but there is a reason she is so revered. I loved your pictures of the cloisters and the view down the cliffs. And I hope you find more atmosphere walking in the hills than at the Briviesca sanctuary. It's fascinating that the oldest human fossils in Europe have been found in La Bureba valley. I wonder if Casilda sensed the history of the cave she settled in?

Maybe you will get more of a feel for her presence in Toledo. Your hamsa came from there when Catherine was searching for her own answers and grieving the loss of Miriam Jacobs.

Write to me soon and be kind to yourself.

Much love always,
Eliška.

Miriam folds the much-read letter back into the envelope stuffed with two years of notes and postcards from Eliška. She slips out of the pew in the Chapel of Saint Ana and through the extravagant Gothic cathedral with its extraordinary dome above the simple slab of dark red marble that marks El Cid's remains.

Outside, she feels a sudden wish for company, shakes herself, turns and collides with...

I'm so sorry, both women apologise, laugh.

You're... sorry, you reminded me of... Who is it that the woman reminds her of? Casilda Faertes, Miriam says, A singer I...

You're a friend of my daughter?

Sorry?

Casilda's my daughter. I'm Miriam, by the way. When did you last see her?

You're... Of course, that's why you look so alike. Miriam laughs again. I'm Miriam too. I don't really know Casilda, but I met her after a concert she gave in Toledo in the spring. Her music is extraordinary.

Casilda's mother nods. It is. Talented and driven and doesn't know when to stop. She's on tour in the States now, no doubt giving them lectures on social justice at the end of every concert.

Ah, yes. She gave a passionate plea for the role of music in culture when I heard her play, but I liked it. Too many people walk around asleep.

You sound just like her. She's definitely not asleep. All her life I've told her, don't go looking for trouble, Casilda, find another way, but she is who she is...

Quixote?

Yes. And well spotted. But I'm keeping you talking in this hot street when anyone sane would be indoors. It marks us out as foreigners. Come and have coffee with me.

You're not Spanish?

Me? Hungarian. Not that I remember the place. I grew up

in Nice but I've been here more than forty years. Come, my house is round the corner...

As they walk, Casilda's mother says, You know, you remind me of someone too, a woman I met in Nice when I went back after my grandmother's funeral. She was English, lost in the Chagall paintings, overwhelmed by them, in fact, or by whatever they'd reminded her of. A little older than you perhaps, but otherwise, you might be her.

In the stone house, painted a distinctive shade of chartreuse, the tint of Anjou pears and the only house on Calle Santa Águeda among the blocks of low-rise apartments, they enter an elegant kitchen, cool tiled floor and hefty wooden table.

Miriam hears a whisper: *Casilda*, and turns, the scent of oranges flooding her senses, tries to catch a shadow moving but the vision to her left is blank, a dark void ringed in a pulsing halo.

Oh...

For pity's sake, Simon, what are you saying?

Eliška's voice is brittle, full of fear. She hears her father mumble a reply but can't make out the words.

She is not Catherine. Eliška's words are punched out, slow, emphatic.

I know that. Of course I do. I didn't mean I'd... It's just... Oh, God, Eliška. She ran away from me. She...

Shh. Don't torture yourself. You scared her but she'll be fine. She's... sensitive.

Like Catherine.

Like, yes… but…

But she is…

Simon, don't. You have to get some perspective.

God always demands a sacrifice, Casilda. She hears the words out loud, sits up in bed and flashes on the light. Of course there is no-one there, she tells herself. Must have been dreaming, she says to the empty room. She shivers. There's no central heating in the cottage in Harlech. Miriam loves the wood burning stoves, but in December the pile of blankets over her duvet feels like a weight crushing her.

She snuggles down in the dark. No central heating, no noise of traffic, no television, no school. She learnt Welsh from the children who play in the local streets, just as she learnt Czech from Eliška and German from Simon. Catherine spoke French and Italian, but she knows them only a little, from CD courses that she finds dry and dull. She wants to learn Spanish, to travel in search of the stories of Saint Casilda that her mother left behind.

Her mother was religious when she was young, Simon has told her. There is no religion here. Simon and Uncle Nathan are Jewish in culture only. Yet notions of the occult are never far from Simon's work and thoughts, as though he is always searching for belief, but never able to allow it. Belief was Catherine's gift, he has told her. Eliška is open to what she calls 'something out there' and Miriam is fascinated by her aunt's studies in Kabbalah. One day she will study the Sufism that Casilda and Ben Haddaj might have known before they converted, one to a new tradition, one going back to his ancestors. She drifts back into sleep, but in her dreams the voice is insistent: God always demands a sacrifice, Casilda.

December 6 2006 is a Wednesday. She wakes knowing that the instant she lifts the covers she will be shivering. She feels groggy from a night of strange dreams. She grabs a thick sweater and pulls it over the baggy flannel shirt she wears for bed, hauls on tie-dyed yoga trousers and woollen socks before heading down the two flights to the kitchen. She can hear Eliška's voice in the living room and smiles, glad her aunt is staying with them for a while before she returns to Prague, though she's sad that Eliška and Uncle Nathan are separating. The answering voice is not Simon's and Miriam wonders who could be visiting so early. Or has she slept late? She opens the door to the living room a crack and Eliška turns towards her, face tear-streaked and puffy. The man seated in the chair opposite Eliška half stands.

Miriam, come in, he says softly and Eliška chokes back a sob.

Miriam stands in the doorway looking from Eliška to the man. She's seen him before, but...

Doctor Roberts?

Miriam moves towards Eliška, who stands and hugs her tight, pulling her to sit beside her on the sofa.

Eliška? What is it? Where's Simon?

The choke becomes a wail and Doctor Roberts moves forward, squats beside them.

Sorry, I'm... I'll be fine... I... Eliška swallows tears, brushes a hand across her face. Miriam, she begins. Simon's... Simon's not... I mean...

She looks at Doctor Roberts who opens his mouth to deliver the news, but Eliška shakes her head, starts again. Simon took his life, Miriam. He was... You know he's been struggling. You know he loved you very much, but it's been so hard for him without Catherine and recently... it seemed harder recently...

Took his life, Miriam echoes weakly. You mean he...

I'm afraid your father died in the early hours of this morning, Miriam, Doctor Roberts says, putting a firm hand on her arm.

But how?

He took sleeping pills, he says simply.

But Simon hated pills. He didn't use... Did you give those to him? Her voice is ragged, angry.

Miriam... Eliška begins, but Doctor Roberts holds up a hand.

No, Miriam, I didn't know your father had them. The drug he took used to be prescribed for insomnia sometimes, but it's very dangerous, rarely prescribed except by vets these days.

But where did he... She trails away.

Maybe while he was on his reading tour in the States, Eliška answers. Two Australian doctors wrote a book about using it for assisted suicides and euthanasia just recently. There was a lot of media attention...

It's a very strong barbiturate, Doctor Roberts adds.

But don't you have to take loads? Why didn't he throw up? How could he take so many?

Miriam, Eliška begins again, I know you'll have lots of questions, but...

But how could it happen? Miriam demands, her voice louder than she ever remembers hearing it.

Doctor Roberts squeezes her arm. Ten grams of this powdered in water, just a small cup of water, is enough. That's what makes it so dangerous. But not painful, he adds. It's known as the peaceful pill.

But he wasn't feeling peaceful, was he?

No, Miriam, I'm afraid he can't have been. I'm sorry. Doctor Roberts stands and flexes. There are people on their way who will take the… who will take your father …

Take him where? What people?

Undertakers, Eliška whispers. There has to be an inquest, darling. He…

Miriam nods. Thank you for telling me all of this, she says to Doctor Roberts, holding her voice almost steady. Did he… Was there a note?

Eliška reaches into a pocket and smooths out a folded slip of pale blue paper. On it is written: God always demands a sacrifice, Casilda.

She stands, is overwhelmed by the reek of rotting lilies and over-ripe oranges, lights dancing in a halo around a black void, sways and…

Miriam! Thank goodness, I… Are you alright? Stupid question. Don't move.

Miriam sits up on the beautiful tiled floor of the kitchen, trying to remember where she is. Her left temple pulses with pain and she feels sick, but the black void has moved away and the smell of oranges is gone.

I'm so sorry, she says. I'll be fine. I get these migraines occasionally.

I shouldn't have kept you talking in the sun, Casilda's mother chides herself. Here. She helps Miriam into a chair. I'll be back with water. Anything else?

Water's fine.

My mother used to get migraines, Casilda's mother tells her when she returns with the water in a cobalt blue glass. I don't remember her, but Grand-maman said she would smell oranges and have optical hallucinations.

I have the same sensations, Miriam whispers, taking the glass. I don't remember my mother either. She died giving birth to me.

How sad. Terrible. Mine died in prison after the Uprising. She was executed just months before there was a policy shift… My grandmother… anyway, that's a story for another day.

Your mother was imprisoned after the '56 Uprising? How strange. Mine was in Budapest in '93, researching a woman in prison for a novel she wrote. Selene, she was called…

Casilda's mother blanches. Selene Solweig Virág, she says. My mother was Selene Solweig Virág.

Miriam Virág

I'm sure you will know this for yourself—some people are vampires.

Charming, educated, an artist with a big laugh who loved to throw parties, Rafael enchanted me. I came to Zaragoza in a daze after the nun-like seclusion of six years of dancing school, varied only by teaching dance to children and teenagers. My world had shrunk and my naïvety had risen. Having grown up gregarious, I was hungry for culture and for company and, although Zaragoza was a small city, it was lively and welcoming. I was indefatigable in my search for new music and experimental film, for art and people, especially when they came with a hint of the radical or intellectual about them. There were a few men in the early days, but they soon showed themselves dull or possessive or both. And then there was Rafael.

You look gorgeous staring off into the sunset like that. That was the first thing he said to me, at a party in a small art gallery. I should paint you.

Yet it didn't begin well. Having told me how gorgeous I was, Rafael leant in, large hand on the nape of my neck beneath my hair, pulled me towards him, mouth seeking mine. I gasped, twisted, teeth clattering against his, jerked back shaking my head. I had a flash of one of those detailed and grotesque Goya etchings I'd seen recently. But Rafael only laughed and invited me to have dinner with him the next day.

When he said goodbye to me later that evening, after what turned out to be his opening show, he added, This is the start of the story.

Did I mention I'm having dinner with Luisa?

What? I thought she'd gone back to Madrid?

She did, but she hated her new boss. She's staying with a friend while she looks for a new flat, but it's a bit cramped. I thought she could stay with us instead...

No.

What do you mean?

No, she can't.

It's my flat, Miriam. Anyway, don't be childish.

I spent an afternoon on a bench outside what had once been a synagogue, but was now a seminary. Every time we argued I railed at myself for giving up my lovely attic studio at the top of 15 Calle Santa Cruz. I sat pondering, convincing myself that Rafael was right, that I was being silly. I wandered the streets where the Christian and Jewish areas had been separated by gates in the early Middle Ages. In Plaza San Gil, along Calle de San Lorenzo and in Plaza Magdalena, I imagined a city that had once had a Jewish castle, a hospital, butchers' shops and synagogues. It was not religion that separated me from Rafael, but there was something unbridgeable between us nonetheless, perhaps because I was so uncertain of who I was or wanted to be.

Sometimes I would tell him that I wanted to leave, but he always retorted that I was being ridiculous.

You don't know what you want, he used to tell me, and I found it hard to argue with that.

I knew he was having affairs. 'Knew' in the sense that I constantly denied it to myself, but I started having headaches, feeling unable to get out of bed in the morning, sometimes closing the studio for days, once for a whole week because I couldn't face the world.

I was stubborn, constantly believing I could change him. But one night at a party, another of his exhibitions, I watched him fawning over Luisa, got very drunk and went home with one of Rafael's followers. Javier was also an artist, a thin young man with large eyes and a soft voice, who had comforted me too many times before. Ironically, I didn't even sleep with him. Perhaps I was too drunk and, in any case, Javier worshipped Rafael.

I have no idea how many women Rafael had slept with in our five years together, only that it was many, but he threw me out the next morning, mocking the idea that I could have stayed overnight with Javier without having sex.

For a while I slept in the studio, once again wishing I had not moved out of the attic above it. I could have thrown myself on Javier's mercy, but I knew I wasn't in love with him, so it seemed cruel. I told myself I'd look for a new apartment soon, but I couldn't shake the story of Saint Casilda that I'd heard in Toledo and decided, rather naïvely, to set off for Burgos to learn more about her. I left with little more than I'd arrived with, except for you, my own Casilda, my daughter and Rafael's daughter, tucked safely inside me.

The Circle is Small

August 2018

Small world indeed, Casilda says. She reaches a hand across the table and rests it on Miriam's arm. Mamá is still reeling from discovering that your mother wrote a novel about Selene.

Catherine dreamt her, dreamt Selene's life I mean, Miriam says, wondering at what point these people will decide she's insane.

Casilda nods. And what happened to your mother?

She died when I was born... I...

Do you think she... I mean that you and she... Casilda laughs. Sorry, it's all very strange, but I'm glad you're here. She squeezes Miriam's arm and stands, begins pacing her mother's kitchen, bare feet on the cool tiles of the floor.

I kept thinking about you after we played at El Tránsito. Your boyfriend seemed determined to get you away quickly.

We weren't together long, Miriam says. I should have just said I was going to eat at La Abadia and let him follow or not.

Casilda nods. But we'd met before and I had this weird feeling that you were...

Casilda? The eleventh century one? Miriam asks.

Yes.

Casilda's mother enters and puts her hands on her daughter's shoulders. Stop pacing, sweetheart, you'll wear us all out. She gazes into her daughter's face. Your eyes are too dark, not getting enough sleep.

Casilda laughs, hugs her mother and moves back so that they stand, each with their hands on the the other's shoulders. Touring is exhausting, Mamá. And America is… so big, so fast, so much… I couldn't live there, but there's an extraordinary energy. Anyway, I'll sleep in my own bed tonight and you can feed me.

Miriam Virág nods and goes to the oven, from where the scent of almonds, lamb and paprika is escaping. You can open a tinto fino to go with this, she says, bending to lift the blue and white glazed tagine onto the stovetop.

Basconcillos, Casilda says, I've already opened one.

Ah, that's my daughter. She puts the tagine onto the tiled middle of the wooden kitchen table and winks at Miriam.

To Selene and Catherine, Miriam Virág toasts when they are all seated and the plates heaped with fragrant stew, chunks of still-warm homemade bread on the side plates.

Miriam lifts her glass and echoes the toast.

Casilda smiles, glancing from her mother to the woman who has once again wandered into her life. She takes a forkful of food and chews slowly.

So Catherine was in Budapest in 1993 and started to dream

Selene's life? Casilda asks at last.

Miriam nods. I don't know how, but it seems that what she wrote was fairly accurate. She found documents about Selene's birth and also met the son of the man who'd shared a gallery with Selene's parents in Paris.

Grand-maman, that's Marie, took me there, Miriam Virág says wistfully. But she wouldn't go in. She cried in the street and then we walked away again.

The people at the gallery kept Sándor's sketchbook for years, Miriam says. They wanted to find the family and when my mother turned up they gave it to her. They asked her to give it to Selene's daughter if she found her.

And she never did find me, but you have. Do you have it still?

Miriam nods. At home in Prague. It's beautiful. The picture of Selene as a child especially. She looks... Miriam takes a gulp of the rich red wine. She looks like my mother looked in pictures as a child. It's...

Unfathomable, Casilda puts in. She rubs her arms. I know it's insane but I just felt so cold for a second when I said that. I think this meal needs more wine.

Miriam Virág nods and Casilda walks to the rack, levers a cork from another local Basconcillos and leaves it standing on the kitchen surface. It's not the only one that needs to breathe, she quips, returning to the table.

I don't think it's just the sketchbook or that Catherine knew your mother's life, Miriam says after they've sat in silence a few minutes. The other two look up, expectant. The details... the birth and where Selene lived and facts about Marie and Sándor in Paris and that Selene was in prison... I mean, even if Catherine dreamt all that, those things could be checked to some extent, but there was something else... you'll understand if you read the novel, of course...Miriam pauses, breathes deeply, begins again. Selene thought... I mean she believed that... She puts her hands on the table and gazes at Casilda's mother. You told me that when your mother was executed, all she left behind was a scrap of a poem by Attila József and a tiny damascene hamsa.

Yes, Miriam Virág says, that's correct. Her voice hoarse and quiet.

Selene believed that Attila József was your father, that at moments when she was under stress or experienced migraines she found herself somehow taken back to 1937 during the last month of Attila's life. I know it doesn't make sense, but...

Miriam Virág drains her glass and looks intently at Miriam, whispers, And the hamsa?

Miriam fingers the tiny talisman at her throat. She nods and drains her own glass. My mother wrote about it in her journal. She found it by her bed when she visited Toledo in search of the original Princess Casilda. By then her friend had died. She was also called Miriam, the one who believed she'd been Ben Haddaj of Zaragoza in a former life. While she was in Toledo, my mother was ill one day, bleeding, and she dreamt that her friend, Miriam Jacobs, was there with her. When she woke, the hamsa was by her side. Later, she realised that she'd seen Judith, Miriam's mother, wearing it years before. What she couldn't work out was how it got from Selene to Judith, but...

Judith was Grand-maman's niece, Miriam Virág says. And she named her daughter for me. Grand-maman must have given it to my great-aunt Hélène when she thought she'd have no-one to leave it to. But Hélène died before Grand-maman, so it would have passed to Judith and then...

Time for that second bottle, Casilda cuts in, glancing at the empty glasses as she scrapes back her chair.

You should have this, Miriam says when Casilda sits down again. She holds out the hamsa, but Casilda and Miriam Virág shake their heads in unison.

It came to you, Miriam Virág says.

Because it belongs with Casilda, Casilda adds. And, confusingly, it seems that you are Casilda, the original one I mean, not me.

Miriam looks from mother to daughter. You believe all this?

Miriam Virág shrugs, but says, I can't see any other option. Grand-maman told me again and again how ancient this hamsa is and how the man who sold it to her mother in Toledo sensed it wanted to go to her family. Perhaps it was finding its way to my mother, to Selene. And then to Catherine and to you. Perhaps it goes all the way back to the first Casilda of Toledo.

I've written that in my novella, Miriam says quietly. But...

Because it's probably as true as it is insane, puts in Casilda. But then, too much sanity may be madness...

Miriam smiles. Catherine wrote that many times in her journals. And that the unreason of the world really is more insane than any fiction.

Casilda refills their glasses and lifts her own. To Casilda of Toledo and Ben Haddaj of Zaragoza, elusive as he has been, and to all who refuse to surrender dreams. And to us. May we see life as it is, and not as it should be.

Glasses clink and the women lapse into silence, mopping at the last traces of meat-juice with the remains of the bread.

Almond cake and orange sauce, Miriam Virág says finally. Before a good night's sleep. She smiles at Miriam. The woman I said you reminded me of when I first met you — in the Chagall Museum in Nice, when I returned after Grand-maman died — could it have been Catherine?

Miriam nods. She was there for work in July '91.

So she found me after all, but too early, Miriam Virág says. A very small world indeed.

Miriam Virág

And so to Burgos. I have no idea why I had become fascinated with the story of a Muslim princess who became a Christian saint and who might have been loved (unrequited as it was) by a Jewish prince, who appeared to the world to be a Muslim. But something about the story tugged at me. Perhaps it was no more than the notion that we can always reinvent ourselves that resonated so deeply. A Hungarian who knew nothing of her own country, who felt French, but lived in Spain, needed unusual role models after all.

It was an odd place to wash up for a young Jewish single mother. The synagogue in Burgos, apparently once a small building in the parish of San Miguel next to a fortified house, had disappeared centuries before. In the thirteenth century, Rabbi Meir Halevi Abulafia and the poet Todros Halevi Abulafia lived there, illuminating Hebrew manuscripts, adding to Kabbalah. By 1412 the synagogue was expropriated and the Jews confined to a Jewish quarter following the laws of Ayllón. It was ever thus. The city of El Cid was no resting place for Jews, even if they had financed his military campaigns with their loans.

Where did they disappear to? They left hardly any artefacts — only a hanukkiah, a few pieces of pottery, fewer silver plates, decorated with six-pointed stars, are on display at the Burgos Museum.

Conversion was always an option in hard times. After the civil war of the mid fourteenth century, the Jewish community was stripped of its wealth, could no longer make loans to Christians and suffered attacks. The Seville Massacre in June 1391 began a wave of killings that spread to Burgos and soon Paul of Burgos had converted. A rabbi and Talmudic scholar, revered for his piety and wisdom, was baptised with his brothers and children, though his wife, Joanna, held out till her death. Paul, aka Salomon Ha-Levi, became Bishop Pablo de Santa María and took an active role in persecuting Spanish Jewry. Another of his extended family founded the synagogue of El Tránsito in Toledo, whilst another, Luis de Carvajal, returned to Judaism only to be executed by the Inquisition.

The madness of the world…

And yet, I felt oddly at home in Burgos. You grew within me and I took a job working in the art exhibitions section at the Museo de Burgos. I lived like a nun, as I had in Barcelona, and saved every peseta that didn't go on rent or food so that I would not have to work when my baby was born. I never contacted Rafael again, and sometimes I have regretted that, but I gave you his surname so that you would be at home in this country.

You were five when I met Isak. Tall, talented and gentle, he was the first lover I'd had who was also a friend. And, of course, he adored you. A storyteller, linguist and musician, he taught violin, guitar and nyckelharpa, whilst I once again set up my own dance studio. I saw no need to send you to nursery or preschool. You met local children at dance and music classes and by the time you were six and had began your primer ciclo school years, I was proud of your fluency in Hungarian, French and Spanish. You were already learning Swedish and English, could dance and were beginning to play your own nyckelharpa, built to size by Isak, as well as learning violin from him.

My darling girl, you were such an easy child, sunny and bright, and suddenly life seemed simple. We moved from an apartment to a whole house, finally dipping into the wealth that Grand-maman had left me. Only a few streets from my dance studio, it had arched windows in the bedrooms that looked down onto a little square of Calle Santa Águeda and adjoined the next door church, with its plaque bearing the legend that here, Rodrigo Díaz de Vivar, better known as El Cid, forced King Alfonso VI of León to swear that he had not taken part in the murder of his brother, Sancho II, Rodrigo's lord. However fictional the story, I liked living next to somewhere that had stood so long, older than the lavish Gothic cathedral at the top of the road, and I liked the idea of El Cid, who had known exile, sold his services to protect Moorish taifa and eventually ruled over a Valencia that was a haven for Christians and Muslims alike.

I was also amused that the church had been home to a namesake of your father. Rafael Arnáiz Barón, born on Saint Casilda's day in 1911. He was an intense young man who desperately wanted to take Trappist monastic vows, but was prevented by his severe diabetes, from which he died aged only twenty-seven. But he'd left a legacy of extraordinary spiritual letters and had been beatified before we moved into Calle Santa Águeda and was finally canonised in November 2006, just before your own life also changed.

You were fourteen when Isak left and it was hard for all of us. My lover had become more my friend with every year and, much as he adored you, he wanted more than companionship. He hoped to father a child and I had no need to mother another. I know you missed him even more than me. I remember all the postcards you wrote to one another and the mobile phone he sent for your fifteenth birthday, a tiny Motorola V3 that you delighted in flipping open.

December 6 2006 was a Wednesday. You were nearing the end of your first term studying for the bachillerato. You seemed to breeze through life, happily studying history, Spanish and English, but delighting most in the arts. At sixteen you showed no sign of any romantic interest, but had good friends, particularly Isabella, who I'd been teaching dance to since she was four.

It was a cold day, rain pattering on the roof as I woke, but I was soon aware of another sound, a strange, low moaning. I roused and ran to your room.

Darling, what is it?

You were sitting up in bed, rocking and crying.

Casilda?

You looked at me as though struggling to work out who I was. I felt your head and it was cold, but covered in sticky sweat.

Does it hurt? Can you tell me?

You struggled to focus on me and only wailed louder.

The doctor could find nothing wrong, but your world changed that day.

It became a dark place for you, one you felt was filled with dishonesty and injustice. I remember every moment of the weeks you refused to leave your bedroom, barely leaving your bed.

And, of course, it took Isak to convince you, at last, that you could take the world on if you chose.

To change the world, my friend, is not madness, or utopia, but justice, he wrote to you.

And he kept saying it into the phone whenever you would answer. And so, Quixote-like, you got up to take on the world. And if it was only tilting at windmills, I was at least grateful that you had a purpose in life again. But I ache still that you have continued to struggle with depression, despite your passions for music and justice. I wonder still what happened that day to my bright, happy girl.

I'm Not Supposed to Care

August 2018

Come with me, Casilda says for at least the tenth time that day.

I'm supposed to be going back to Prague.

To do what?

I don't know yet. We're going round in circles. I don't know…

… how all this is going to work out, Casilda finishes for her.

Miriam nods.

You could work anywhere. Don't go and bury yourself in some fusty archive. Write your novella. Get a book deal. Two book deals—the novella and the nonfiction.

Miriam laughs. Oh yes, the world is queuing up for books on the influence of Sufism on Kabbalah and how they translate into motifs within fiction. And as for the novella… I'm not sure it's…

I'll be sure for you, Casilda objects. Belief used to your gift, my darling, Casilda.

Sorry? Miriam shakes herself. Did you say something else or am I hearing your thoughts? I seem constantly to lapse into other versions of ourselves, she says. Are we insane?

Only if we let each other go. I have this strong sense that this is our last chance. Don't go back to Prague.

Miriam puts her head in her hands and says nothing.

Phone Eliška, Casilda urges. Talk to her. From what you've told me, she'll understand. You came here looking for Casilda, and you've found her. In fact, you are her! And I'm your Ben Haddaj. No more losing one another. Casilda pauses, sighs. Please, Miriam.

OK, I'll call Eliška, Miriam says after a while. I need to phone today, anyway. It's... I mean it would have been my mother's birthday. She would have been 57.

Casilda springs from her seat, puts her arms around Miriam. An omen!

What do you mean?

The day you came to my concert, back in April, that would have been Selene's birthday.

Miriam begins to cry, thick sobs choking her as Casilda rocks her. When the tears finally subside she looks up at Casilda's anxious face, the dark curls fallen across it. I can't bear to think that my life's predestined, she says shakily. If we'd just met and... but all this... I... she gestures vaguely, begins to cry again, more softly.

But we're not. It's not like that. We set this up ourselves. Generations ago maybe, but no-one did this to us. You weren't ready for love, you had a spiritual quest, and I wasn't free to love you. And somehow we've gone on searching for each other and missing each other, for so many reasons. But now…

They both remain silent, seconds becoming long minutes.

If you don't want it… Casilda says at last. There's another pause. But if you do, don't leave me. We can work out the logistics, that's all this is… as long… as long as you want it…

After the call, during which Eliška has reassured her, over and over, that she will always have a home in Prague, but really, if she loves this girl, she must… Miriam mutters that she needs to walk, to think. It's late afternoon and she wanders the streets of Burgos, finding herself outside the cathedral, where she had first bumped into Miriam Virág. She wants to slip inside, feel the cool air wash over her, but the cathedral can only be entered by way of the tourist shop that sells tickets. She pays the €7 and walks to the tomb of El Cid, the simple slab beneath the lantern of light from the exquisite octagonal dome above.

Did you really meet Casilda? She asks the floor. Or were you too late? Too late, she thinks. But perhaps you met Zoraida, maybe as Isabel, wife of Alfonso. And you fought for the Muslim prince of Zaragoza, though among their names I can find no Prince Ben Haddaj, only connections to connections… And you ruled over a Valencia of Christians and Muslims living well together for a while. She lays a hand on the cold stone. Was Ben Haddaj a vizier, nephew to a vizier? An alchemist? A myth? And what has any of this to do with me? Why am I asking a long dead icon? And should I stay with Casilda?

There are no answers. She wishes there were votive stands, a place to drop coins into a box and light a creamy white candle, but this is no longer a house of prayer except on great occasions like Corpus Christi. Happy birthday, Catherine, she whispers, I'll light you a candle this evening.

December 6 2006 is a Wednesday. She wakes knowing that the instant she lifts the covers she will be shivering. She feels groggy from a night of strange dreams... she stands in the doorway looking from Eliška to a man she's seen before, but... Where's Simon? You know he loved you very much, but it's been so hard for him without Catherine and... But Simon hated pills. He didn't use... Where did he... how could it happen? A note... Was there a... Eliška reaches into a pocket and smoothes out a folded slip of pale blue paper. *God always demands a sacrifice, Casilda.*

December 6 2006 was a Wednesday, Miriam Virág had said to her. Casilda was nearing the end of her first term studying for the bachillerato. She was sixteen. It was a cold day, rain pattering on the roof, and she could hear a low moaning. Casilda was sitting up in bed, rocking and crying. She looked at me as though she didn't know who I was, Miriam Virág had told her. And she was cold, but covered in sweat. The doctor could find nothing wrong with her... But she changed that day. The world became a dark place for her...

A dark place, Miriam says to no-one.

He's been in her dreams since she was twelve years old. The beach goes on forever... He puts an arm around her shoulder... There is a movement so small, so strange... She pulls away, begins to run...

And later, trying to overhear the conversation, Eliška's voice brittle and afraid. Her father mumbling a reply she can't make out... *She is not Catherine.* She is like her, yes... but... And her father sobbing and saying: *But she is...*

God always demands a sacrifice, Casilda.

Miriam turns and sees Casilda standing behind her.

You've been hours, Casilda says. Are you okay?

Miriam nods. Just thinking. How did you know where I'd be?

Just a guess. Mamá said she first met you coming out of here. She smiles. Not too Jewish.

My mother was a Catholic, though not practising when she married Simon.

I think we found each other for a while in them, Casilda replies. If you hadn't died in childbirth my life would never have changed the day Simon killed himself. It is the same day isn't it?

Miriam nods.

So here we are, together again. She holds out a hand and Miriam takes it.

Will you stay?

Miriam nods. I'll come with you on tour at least. I can use the time to write book proposals, but I need to see Eliška after that. Perhaps you can come to Prague with me?

In reply Casilda pulls her close and kisses her mouth. A passing woman sucks in her teeth and mutters something, crossing herself, but Casilda only pulls Miriam closer. Thank you, she whispers.

And by the way, Casilda says, as they walk from the cathedral into the evening sunlight. We're done with sacrifice. I have a feeling I've said this before, though I can't imagine why or where, but sacrifice went out with Amos more than seven hundred years before Christ. Do you know the verses? *But let justice roll down like waters, and righteousness like an everflowing stream. Did you bring to me sacrifices and offerings the forty years in the wilderness, O house of Israel?* She grins. Even Abraham didn't have to sacrifice his own son in the end. God provided an alternative.

Miriam Virág

There has been no-one since Isak and I've been happy with that. You needed a lot of support to find your Quixotic way and I had my dance studio and a full life. Since the diagnosis, my greatest fear has been how to tell you, but now I can do that. It will be hard, and I am terrified that the darkness might creep back for a while, but Miriam will take care of you.

I've written to Isak, who never did have a child of his own, and he's agreed to visit in time for your return from the tour of northern medieval cities. We'll be together for your concert at La Casa de las Musas, a short walk round the corner on Calle Eduardo Martínez del Campo. Later. We'll open a good bottle of Basconcillos and tell you the difficult news before Miriam goes to see her aunt in Prague. You will, in any case, soon guess that something is wrong. Even in the six weeks you've been away, I've grown thinner and my energy is flagging rapidly.

It's good to think of you tonight, performing in Toledo, at your favourite Santa Maria la Blanca, though you would, of course, tell me that I should call it Ibn Shushan Synagogue. I'll sit in my beautiful kitchen with a glass of tinto fino and drink to my beautiful, driven daughter and the love of your life. I'll toast you, my Casilda, who may once have been Ben Haddaj, a prince of Zaragoza, and later a marvellous Hungarian poet who died under a train only to return as Miriam Jacobs, my cousin's daughter, and as Simon Garrett, Miriam McManus's father. And I'll toast Miriam McManus. This intense young woman my Casilda loves, and who, I believe, was once Santa Casilda, the solitary healer who has fascinated me for years, perhaps because she also lived in the mother I can't remember.

Do the story and the facts have to match? I have no idea. But now I understand why Saint Casilda has always fascinated me. I even have an inkling of what happened to you that awful day in December when Simon died and you took on his mantle. The rest is for you and Miriam to work out, my darling.

I Want to Hear It from You

October 2018

It's in Toledo, leaving Santa Maria la Blanca, (*Ibn Shushan Synagogue*, Casilda always insists) that they run into Mateo.

Miriam! You're… I didn't know you were… I thought you'd be back in Prague… I…

She feels Casilda slip a hand into hers and squeeze, sees Mateo's face tighten.

It would be good to catch up, Mateo says, but his voice is stiff.

We're leaving in the morning, Casilda replies, before Miriam can answer for herself. But good to see you again. Casilda pulls on her arm, but she resists.

We're going to La Abadia, Miriam says. Why don't you join us? She feels Casilda tense and pulls her hand away as Casilda pushes fingernails into her palm.

Mateo glances from one to the other and shakes his head. Just on my way to meet a friend, he says. Girlfriend, he adds. But it was good running into you. He puts his hands on Miriam's shoulders and kisses each cheek lightly. You take care, he says, and walks away.

Bastard! Casilda mutters.

No, he's not... he's just...

Casilda rubs her temple. I think I've got a migraine coming on, she says. Can you smell oranges?

Miriam sighs. No, she says. Let's go and eat. You'll feel better.

But as they walk to La Abadia, Miriam hears a distant whisper: so slight, so small, so brutal that...

The facts and the story must match, she says to Casilda.

Pardon?

You have to trust me.

I...

I'm not going through all that again. Being accused of betrayal, being... If you don't trust me, say so now and I'll go back to Prague.

Miriam begins to cry, big noisy tears.

They stop outside Cristo de la Luz and Casilda throws her arms around her, clinging tightly. You're right, she murmurs. I'm sorry. We've done this dance before. If I'd trusted you, maybe Cassie and Miriam would still be alive together in a small seaside town in England. How do I stop being so insecure?

I'm not sure I know how, Miriam admits. But I know you have to do it.

Yes, Casilda agrees. Or Mateo will be there waiting in the wings when I screw up.

Like Liam, Miriam adds. Though I don't think Mateo is so... Anyway, let's eat.

Wait, one more thing.

Miriam turns to face Casilda. From behind, the tiny mosque throws dappled shadows across them...

A shadow pale as dust flits across a mote of light, the fragrance of roses suffusing the air. Somewhere a string is plucked, faint music —

> *Al-'ūdu qud tarannam*
> *Bi-abdā'i talhīn*
> *Wa ṣaqqod al-madā nib*
> *Riyād al-basātîn*

Miriam shivers.

Not oranges, Casilda says, roses. Can you smell them?

Miriam nods. What was your one more thing?

Casilda leans close. Only that I love you, she says.

Miriam smiles, kisses Casilda and takes her hand. *For hope is always born at the same time as love.*

Part II

In the first part of this story we left the Toledan princess, Casilda, also known as Miriam McManus, and her indefatigable defender, Ben Haddaj, also known as Casilda Faertes, deep in love; Ben Haddaj having realised that he must break the pattern of centuries if he and Casilda were to have any hope of bringing their story to a resolution. And this might be the end of the story, but theirs is an extraordinary encounter; one that in another age minstrels would have sung ballads about; a romance full of adventure that should not be left unwritten.

I'm Not Saying

April 2020

In the story, there is an incident so slight, so small, that no-one except your character, Casilda, and the man who is in love with her, Ben Haddaj, knows exactly what has taken place. But, in offering healing and recognising her belief, Ben Haddaj sacrifices his chance of being with her. A tiny act is all it takes to both unite and overturn their worlds.

Yes, Miriam assents, that's a good assessment.

And your character—Casilda—you've given her your partner's name. Is that significant?

The interviewer leans in.

Well, my character is based on an actual person so it's co-incidence that my partner is also called Casilda. In the case of the book, the original Casilda has become more myth than history. She was a Muslim princess from Toledo in Spain, who became a Catholic saint. What I wanted to explore in the novella was how a young woman from her background could make such a huge transition and how so many myths grew up around her but I also wanted to use fiction to think about the personal cost to someone of becoming an icon.

And is Casilda able to bear this cost?

Ah well, that might be giving too much away. What I can say is that she is someone swept along by a deep belief and a sense of justice. She's at odds with the world she lives in, both its luxury and its conflicts, and also questions her own identity as a Muslim princess.

And that's where Ben Haddaj comes in?

Yes. When she meets Ben Haddaj her young life has already reached a significant crossroads, but this meeting could lead either of them in different directions. Ben Haddaj, who has his own identity struggle, has to face the conundrum that by helping Casilda he will risk the thing he most wants, yet if he doesn't help her... well that would have its own consequences.

And I believe you wrote this novella while working on an MA in Spain, a rather complicated piece of work on the—now let me see if I can get this right—the influence of Sufism and alchemy on Jewish Kabbalah and how themes from those can be traced in contemporary fiction. Am I in the right vicinity?

Miriam laughs. Yes, that's exactly right. Casilda's story is one in which influence from different religious traditions crosses over. It raises questions, a bit like George Eliot's epic poem, *The Spanish Gypsy*. How do we balance loyalty to a particular religious or ethnic identity against more universal claims on our humanity? Moorish Spain is a fascinating setting to explore that question. There was so much crossover of ideas and influence between major religious traditions. And Casilda and Ben Haddaj are at the crux of that, as metaphors, even if their actual history is rather shaky.

David Litton swivels his chair towards the studio audience.

I've been talking to Miriam McManus, author of *Crossing Over*, which is, of course, now available in all good book shops.

He turns back.

Miriam, thank you for being with us this evening and all the best with your book.

Miriam!

She halts. It's dark outside the studio, rain fogging the air.

Miriam!

He is closer now, half way across the road, a tall, dishevelled figure with a smile that has always looked quizzical.

I was in the studio, he says. I wanted to see you. I've read the book. It's... It's amazing, Miriam... I...

Mateo? Is it really you? What are you doing here? I'm... Actually, I'm getting drenched. I...

We could go to a café.

Mateo reaches out to take her arm, but she avoids his touch.

You do know I'm still with Casilda? I'm... You haven't come all this way to...

No, nothing that mad. He grins and flashes a hand bearing a thick band of yellow gold on the third finger. I'm on honeymoon. Well, will be tomorrow. My wife's from London. We were married here last week and I heard about the book and the interview...

That's amazing.

That I got married or that I got over you? He laughs and she laughs with him.

No, the co-incidence I suppose. And congratulations.

You too.

Thank you, me and Casilda aren't married, but…

You could be if you wanted, even in England now.

Marriage is not in Casilda's philosophy, but let's get out of this rain…

I'm not saying you shouldn't stick with her, Mateo says two hours later.

Miriam glances at her watch, realising that she needs to get across London to the little serviced flat she's staying in while she gives interviews and launches the novella.

But you need to get some support for yourself as well, Mateo goes on. She's a strong character and in the circumstances… I know you're strong too, he adds, but differently… more accommodating… and it must be hard for her so soon after…

Miriam nods. We're going to Prague. We'll stay with my aunt Eliška for a while. She's the one who brought me up after my dad died.

He nods. I remember you talking about her. She sounds like an amazing person. He hesitates. But don't you think Casilda might need… I don't know… more professional help?

I'm not sure. Isak, Casilda's stepdad—he thinks she'll pull through with rest and music. I think he may be hatching a plan to get her a tour in Sweden, but not just yet. Maybe she just needs time and love.

What she doesn't say to Mateo is—what really happened when Casilda's mother died, is that Casilda was utterly overwhelmed by darkness. She slept and slept. She doesn't tell him that when Casilda eventually started getting out of bed in the daytime, she was so emotionally exhausted herelf, from writing the novella and worrying about her lover; that she'd lost all track of time; was adrift. She doesn't tell him about living in Miriam Virág's house and feeling so useless or that it was an enormous effort even to persuade Casilda to eat occasionally. And she doesn't mention that she'd told Casilda, over and over: This isn't the end of the story. And had never felt once that Casilda believed her.

Later, in the little flat in central London, she throws open the window, despite the rain, looks across the roofs towards the dome of St Pauls. She will sleep with the windows open behind the shutters so that she can hear the rain in her dreams.

Once there was a Moorish princess, Casilda, daughter of the king of Toledo and a Berber princess, who died in childbirth. She had long golden hair, green eyes, pale skin. She wore only white or the palest blue, almost white like the halo of sky around the sun.

Crossing Over
Miriam Catherine McManus

Chapter 1

Once there was a Moorish princess, Casilda, daughter of the king of Toledo and a Berber girl who died in childbirth. She had long golden hair, green eyes, pale skin. She wore only white or the palest blue, almost white, like the halo of sky around the sun.

A shadow pale as dust flits across a mote of light, the fragrance of roses suffusing the air. Somewhere a string is plucked, faint music—

> *Al-'ūdu qud tarannam*
> *Bi-abdā'i talhīn*
> *Wa ŝaqqod al-madā nib*
> *Riyād al-basatîn*

... a sound of water against stone. Is there a word in the breeze? *Tulaytula.*

Casilda! Casilda!

A thin child with hair that appears to be heavier than her body, looks up. My sister, she whispers.

The man smiles. We can continue tomorrow, he says.

So all material things are laden with manna? Casilda

asks, glancing towards her approaching sister, who is maybe fourteen, wild dark hair tamed by gold threads.

The man nods. As we mix the materials, we bring about transformation. But Zosimos tells us that change must be kairikai.

The right moment?

Yes.

And for Muhammad ibn Umail?

Speak Arabic, Casilda's sister commands, not that Berber babble. She stands with her hands on her hips. You're not still learning poetry, are you? Aren't you bored?

The lute began to resound
with the most beautiful melodies,
and the brooks flowed gaily
through the flower gardens.

What?

It's the poem I've been learning, but we were actually talking about another subject, about…

The other girl shakes her head. Tedious maths then?

Not today, Princess, the man, Abd' Walid al-Waqqal, says, smiling. A little of Sheikh Sahnun, a modicum of rhetoric, more secrets of poetry and a soupçon of alchemy. He bows. But I see Ibn al-Wafid across the garden and have a question for him. If you will excuse me?

Before we finish—Casilda's voice is quiet, but there is an insistence to it. Muhammad Ibn Umail tells us we must go within to seek transformation? The mystery is within the self?

That is so. We are one with all other materials. To be continued, Abd' Walid al-Waqqal says, waving towards Ibn al-Wafid as he strides away.

Zoraida lets out a long sigh to signal her boredom. Come and have something to eat, she says when they are alone. You can't live on poetry and... whatever that was.

We can eat here. Casilda stands and reaches towards a plump apricot.

Better with honey, Zoraida says. But she bites into the fruit Casilda offers. Let's go before they come back, she adds, nodding towards the two men who are now deep in conversation. You'll be learning medicine next from that one.

I would like that, Casilda says. Ibn Wâfid is an extraordinary scholar. He will write great works on simples and sleep, and on curing eye diseases too, but...

How do you know what he will write in the future? Did you dream it?

Casilda nods.

If people knew...

But they don't, Zoraida. And Ibn Wâfid will help me when I'm sick, but...

Sick? You can't get sick. What do you mean? Come and eat. You're too thin and too serious. She takes a deep breath. Please. She reaches out a hand to pull Casilda to her.

Okay, I'll come, but walk through the garden with me first. I love listening to the water running through the pavilion.

Zoraida sighs but nods her agreement.

Majlis an-Naura, Casilda says, stopping in the pavilion.

... there is a rustle of silk, shadows beneath vaulted arches... water bells against stone, whispers, *Casilda*.

Place of water, Zoraida echoes, putting her palm flat onto the cool stone of a spouting lion. I'll grant that your other friend knows how a garden should look.

Ibn Bassal?

Hmm.

It's not just about how it looks. He understands water. How wells have to be near rivers so that water continuously flows in and doesn't fall too low for the chain of pots to reach it. How they must be sunk in August when the water is slow. How to use counterbalances when a chain would become too long. And how...

Enough! You can't really find all this interesting?

But I do. All of it. There will never be another time like this for Toledo and one day...

What? One day what?

Nothing lasts, Zoraida.

But it's not going to change. We're going to keep on having apricots and pomegranates and the wheat will last for seventy years without rotting and the water will flow and the gardens will bloom. And all these stuffy men that father gathers together will go on talking about medicine and maths and law and poetry, and keep on making their weird contraptions, like those...

Like the Astrolabe, Casilda supplies, and all the other beautiful instruments Al-Zarqali makes.

Yes. They are going to go on and on with their talk and inventions for ages and you can learn all of it. Perhaps you'll never even have to marry, but don't run away like that girl in your story. Please... Zoraida begins to cry and Casilda puts thin arms around her.

It's okay, Zoraida. Things change, that's all. But you will be a beautiful queen with beautiful children.

And you?

Casilda shrugs. I will always know I'm loved. She smiles, then clutches her stomach. Oh!

Casilda?

It's nothing, it's...

Oh, you're... Let's get you inside quickly. You know what it is, don't you?

Casilda nods.

Don't worry if it hurts, Zoraida reassures. It's only for a few days each month. It's the first time, isn't it?

Casilda nods again.

As they walk, the air feels cooler, the sky brighter, azure almost white. She has an image of herself in the garden of Mezquita Bab al-Mardum, a rustle of silk, shadows congealing beneath vaulted arches. In the garden water belling against stone, whispers, *Casilda*. And a woman who reminds her of herself, clutches her abdomen and looks up as though she has seen herself a thousand years ago. Unsteady, she glances around. There is no-one with her but Zoraida. She huddles against her sister, feeling the blood ooze through the thin white cotton of her serwal and kamis.

For Lovin' Me

February 2019

Once there was a Moorish princess, Casilda, daughter of the king of Toledo and a Berber princess, who died in childbirth. She had long golden hair, green eyes, pale skin. She wore only white or the palest blue, almost white like the halo of sky around the sun...

She stops reading and looks across at Casilda, unsure of whether she's fallen asleep.

Do you think any of this really happened? Casilda asks.

Yes. And so do you, Miriam replies.

I'm so tired, Miri. Were you...? I mean, did you feel like this when...

When Simon died?

Casilda nods.

I was so young, Miriam says. Only twelve. I was beside myself with grief, but most of it was rage. I couldn't believe he'd do that. I wanted someone to blame. And I felt he'd abandoned me. And at other times I felt like it was my fault.

How could it have been?

There was this day... on the beach. We'd been out walking with Eliška. It was just before she broke up with her husband, Simon's brother—and...

Casilda sits up. What?

I'm not even sure. There was something about the way he hugged me... it... frightened me... and I ran away from him. Later, I heard Eliška and him arguing and I think he said he was afraid of... that he was starting to think of me not as myself, but as Catherine...

God, of course....

There are footprints in the sand. Sand rubbing sand a grain at a time, the world in a grain of sand. Our footprints—large and small, side by side, bare footprints—heel to toe. Sandalled footprints—compact, toeless. Blue sea or grey or green? The sea isn't blue, really, is it? Grey-green. White foam. Scum coloured? Yellow-grey. The sand is golden, or white? The sand is... the beach is a long ribbon of sand, white or gold and... Nothing happened. And in the night I hear Simon crying. I wake up and Eliška is there. And nothing has happened.

I believe in your story, Casilda says, pulling me back to the bedroom. Quixote's right, in a mad world, no fiction can ever be thought of as insane. You only have to pick up a newspaper to see that. But yours is the truth as we lived it. Let's never break the spell again.

I brush a hand across her wild dark hair. We won't.

Even if I never get out of bed?

You will. Your mother wouldn't want you to give up. And Isak won't let you give up. Nor will I.

Yes, she says. And again: Yes. But for now, just a bit more sleep.

If you promise to have some soup later.

She nods, already hunkering under the covers.

In my journal I write:

The story and the facts might match after all. We live inside stories. Tales we tell to make the world safe... to order reality: some false, some true: tales that begin: There are no monsters. Or: Once upon a time, there was a Moorish princess, Casilda...

What really happened was that Casilda's mother died in late January. She told us about the cancer when we returned from Casilda's tour, her second with Bechor Abeidano, Miguel Zapatero and the legendary Zach Buchmann. She'd only felt unwell a few months before, but when she had tests her body was overrun with it, every organ seemed infiltrated.

There's nothing for it but to be stoic, she said.

But surely... Casilda began.

Her mother only shook her head.

How long? I asked quietly.

They said six months to a year, but more likely six months.

And you've known since…? Casilda left the question hanging, went to the wine rack and began uncorking a bottle, splitting the cork and leaving crumbling pieces in the neck. Fuck!

Let me. I took the bottle from her and shepherded her back to a seat at the table before finding glasses, raising the bottle in Miriam's direction in question.

Yes, she said. I can still drink. It's not like I'm having treatment. I've known since August, she said, returning to Casilda's question. I was on my way back from the doctor the day I met Miriam.

Casilda began to wail.

What really happened was that the months from mid October to the end of January were the longest I had ever known, but now they seem to have gone in a moment. I got the offer of two book deals in those strange months, one for my novella and another from an American press that specialised in popularising books bridging philosophy and esotericism.

By then Miriam Virág was weak. She looked like a wraith, but she still led the cheerleading when the letters about my book offers arrived, only two days apart.

You're brilliant, Miriam, I'm so pleased for you. You should phone Eliška. I'm so sorry not meet her.

But she did. Eliška arrived to take care of her in the last weeks and Isak too, though he mostly cooked and fussed over Casilda.

I knew you'd do it, Miriam, Casilda said each time an offer letter arrived.

Even while losing her mother, she was gracious.

Didn't I always say you wouldn't need to work in some fusty archive? she reminded me.

Bechor and Miguel were there for the funeral and played music for the service, Isak filling in for Casilda.

Afterwards, we sat round Miriam Virág's kitchen table and drank too much tinto fino, toasting her and telling stories.

So you're really going? Casilda kept asking Isak and Eliška.

Isak nodded.

I'm afraid I have to get back to work, Eliška said. But you'll come to Prague soon.

And Sweden anytime, Isak added. I promised your mother… Anyway—you know I'm always there for you.

Crossing Over
Miriam Catherine McManus

Chapter 2

How is she, Sulema? Zoraida asks, standing in the doorway of her sister's room.

I'm fine, Casilda calls, despite seeing Sulema shake her head.

Zoraida enters in a cloud of perfume, carrying a long length of silk. Look, she says, kneeling by her sister's divan. I thought you might like this. It's so pale. Ahmed brought beautiful silks back with him.

Casilda fingers the delicate blue fabric. More silks and more prisoners?

I was so worried about you, Zoraida goes on. What if Father had found out?

I suppose he did in a way.

You have to stop going to the dungeons. Next time he might catch you when you're carrying bread. What on earth made you take roses to those filthy prisoners anyway?

I didn't.

But...

It was bread. And then it wasn't.

What do you mean? Do you mean like magic?

Alchemy perhaps.

Isn't that the same?

Real alchemy is when we change within, Zoraida. A great man, Ibn Sina, says that it's through meditation and ecstasy that we are able to change and when we do that then we can also change outward things.

Don't exhaust her, Sulema tells Zoraida, placing a large palm on Casilda's forehead.

You shouldn't let her go to the dungeons, Zoraida retorts. All those foul prisoners. Who knows what diseases they have and...

You know there's no stopping her once she decides one something, Sulema snaps.

Zoraida sighs and perches on the edge of her sister's bed. It has to stop, Casilda. Are you still bleeding?

Yes.

And it started again last night?

Yes.

Maybe this one won't last so long as the others.

Casilda smiles. One of the prisoners told me about a holy well. The waters of San Vicente near Briviesca. The pozo blanco he called it. I will go to the white springs to be cured.

Briviesca? But that's...

The king of Burgos is an ally. It will be fine. But not quite yet. Ahmed hasn't only returned with prisoners. He brought Ben Haddaj too.

Who?

From Zaragoza.

A prince? Is he here as a suitor?

Casilda looks away. Yes, she says, her voice small and distant. He's a suitor in his way, but he's not your future husband.

That's not very exciting then. Perhaps he's ugly?

No, very handsome.

Then why won't he marry me?

Because he's not... it's not the quest he's on.

Ben Haddaj, Prince of Zaragoza. It's not a Muslim name.

Jewish. Ismael, though he hasn't returned to his people yet.

Enough riddles.

Yes. Enough. Sulema ushers Zoraida away. She needs to rest.

Zoraida stands and sticks her tongue out at Sulema.

Insolent girl. Now leave her in peace.

Alone, Casilda drifts into a place of dreams, a place that is not quite sleep. She watches a thin dragon drowning in liquid that is green, then white, but the dragon doesn't die. Instead there is a new creature, a tiny child that looks like a red salamander.

She wakes in blood-soaked sheets and calls out for Sulema.

Oh, my angel! Sulema helps her to stand, peels away the white cotton robe darkened with drying blood. I'll pour you a bath. Let me call that lazy girl to strip the bed. Durra! Durra!

When the bath is ready and Sulema has finished fussing, Casilda sinks into the soothing water, tinged green from the tiles of its surface. She feels the world slipping away, but a familiar voice jolts her.

Casilda! Oh! How are you?

Casilda blinks, pulls herself back from an interior place. She smiles at her sister. I'm fine now. You don't need to worry, Zoraida.

But I saw Durra. She said all your sheets were soaked in blood. And I can see Sulema's been crying.

There's no need to worry about me. Remember I told you how everything changes?

Yes, but... I don't understand why things have to change or what it has to do with bleeding like this. You're so ill, Casilda. You're...

I'm changing, that's all.

You mean into a woman?

Casilda laughs. No. Not that. Into... sometimes things have to come apart to be remade into something new... I've got these different parts — my body and soul and my will. They have to work together, but first they have to be... re-ordered, I suppose.

Zoraida pulls a stool close to the bath and slumps onto it. I have no idea what you are talking about, little sister.

I'm not sure I know how to describe it. It's like I'm waking up, but to do that... I have to... She hesitates and Zoraida leans closer, waiting. I have to be remade and that means pulling some things apart. My soul has to let go of my body and join with my will. Eventually my soul and will and body will join together as one and I'll be... healed.

You won't be sick anymore?

It might not be... I mean it might not look like healing... Not in this life, but...

No! You mustn't talk like that!

I'm sorry. Don't be sad for me. You will be a great queen. And I will work on becoming what is needed of me.

You mean you'll be well?

All shall be well, Casilda says, closing her eyes and sinking deeper into the water. But let me rest now.

Ribbon of Darkness

February 2019

It was after the funeral, after Miguel and Bechor had made a tearful parting and Isak and Eliška had returned to Gothenburg and Prague, that Casilda unravelled.

We're all so scattered, she said in a quiet monotone, sitting at Miriam Virág's kitchen table, left scoured and pristine by Isak. Miguel and Bechor are playing at a festival in Granada and they'll probably get snapped up by some other group while they're there. And there's no point Isak saying I can go to Sweden any time. I can hardly be bothered to walk from one end of the house to the other. I suppose you'll leave me next.

No, of course not. I can write anywhere. Like you said. We'll go to Prague in the spring. Maybe Isak will come too.

Why would he?

Oh, I don't know… I just wondered… I got the impression they…

Isak and Eliška?

Possibly.

Casilda almost smiled, but said only, I need to sleep.

Of course. I'll bring you a drink in a while and cook dinner later.

I don't think I can eat. My head hurts. Can you smell oranges?

When I took a glass of water and a pot of mint tea to her bedroom half an hour later, Casilda was lying still, her eyes glazed, sticky-cold sweat filming her pallid face.

I knelt by the bed. Casilda, Casilda, can you hear me?

There was a moan so low I might have imagined it.

After the doctor's visit, I took up watch at her bedside, writing on a little fold-up table while she slept, reading to her when she woke. Sometimes she would raise a weak smile, but most days I phoned Eliška and Isak to report: No change.

Each day through the rest of February, day after day, week after week of March: No change.

Casilda sleeps and sleeps, olive skin, hair a tangle of soot and pitch. We have known so many defeats across centuries but I wonder how I could go on if I lost her now.

God, it would be the end of the story.

I can't go on, she says to the empty street later when she makes a foray for fresh vegetables.

*

The curtain is pulled across the windows of Casilda's room. Miriam halts in the doorway, the room is stale, the sour tang of cold sweat and shuttered air, and she cannot hear the sound of breathing. God, this is the end... God, please don't let Casilda...

She crosses the room and throws back the cover, feels a wave of nausea.

Casilda!

I'm here, Miriam.

She turns to Casilda, who wavers in the doorway. Her hair looks thin and lank, she's pale, more yellow than olive, but she is standing, beckoning Miriam. Can we go into the garden? I need to breathe.

Miriam begins to cry and Casilda moves forward. Her steps are tentative, but she wraps her arms round Miriam.

Silly Miriam, she says quietly.

And Miriam embraces her, kisses her, laughs.

Crossing Over
Miriam Catherine McManus

Chapter 3

Come in and welcome, Ismael Ben Haddaj, nephew of Vizier Hasdai of Córdoba.

Ben Haddaj flinches. You...?

I'm good at keeping secrets.

Her voice is small. She looks like a bird made of twigs, peering from the white woollen blanket. Her green eyes are greyed and dark rimmed.

My brother and father think you are the Caliph: Prince Ismael Ben Haddaj of Zaragoza. Is it a fiction you have told them or did you work a glamour?

Her voice is amused, encouraging.

He takes a deep breath and nods. As you say, my uncle is the rather well-known Hasdai, who has become Vizier to the Caliph of Córdoba.

Also known as Abu Yusuf ben Yitzhak ben Ezra or Ibn Shaprut, a physician, diplomat, and scientist who is fluent in Hebrew, Arabic and the high language of Latin.

Yes.

And discoverer of Al-Faruk.

Ben Haddaj nods again. You are very well informed, princess. Is it research or by your own magic?

Casilda laughs. He's a famous man and I have excellent teachers. I know he's so gifted and wise that he's become Vizier in all but name and even makes alliances on the Caliph's behalf. And I know he's a renowned botanist. My teachers Ibn Wâfid and Ibn Bassal admire him enormously.

Research then.

She smiles. Not entirely.

Ben Haddaj grins. And I suppose you also know that I'm in love with you?

Casilda turns away. This is not our time, she whispers.

I knew you would think that. Of course, I'd like to change your mind, but I know I won't. I've brought your cure anyway.

She smiles.

We don't have long, he says. It's a little piece of alchemy of course.

Casilda nods. Enough to see me to Burgos.

He leans in, presses something into the palm of her hand and whispers.

Casilda falls back onto the pillows as the door bursts open.

My daughter! Alaman has his hands around Ben Haddaj's throat as Casilda sits up.

I'm so hungry, she says. Could I have some fruit? I'd like to walk in the garden. It's such a lovely day.

Alaman releases Ben Haddaj and scoops up his child.

Once there was a Berber princess, Casilda, wife of the king of Toledo, who died in childbirth. She had long golden hair, green eyes, pale skin. She wore only white or the palest blue, almost white, like the halo of sky around the sun.

Alaman has never made peace with her loss. All he has of her is this frail girl who bleeds and bleeds. And people whisper that his darling child is a traitor, that she smuggles food and medicine to his stinking, festering enemies in the dungeons.

Last night he thought he would break when he found her there on the steps to the dank cages, her robe held up to carry...

What are you doing here?

Surely, he'd thought, she is too weak to be here, on these cold, dark stairs. She has been sick again and...

What are you carrying? He could hardly bear to ask the question. The words come out guttural and hoarse.

Roses, she said, crumpling into unconsciousness.

How had he caught her? He can't remember the movement, the bound down hard steps to prevent her head from slamming into stone. There was barely any weight to carry back to her room.

And now there is this strange new friend of Ahmed's, who insisted he could heal her.

I bring a gift from a most renowned doctor, Abu Yusuf ben Yitzhak ben Ezra, also known as Hasdai. I need only a few moments with the princess. But it must be alone.

Desperation had won over suspicion, but the few moments stretched out, unbearable, until he had burst in...

And here she is, sitting up, asking for food, wanting to go for a walk. And the blood? It is too delicate a question to ask, but...

It's stopped, Casilda says, cutting into his thoughts. So unnerving when she does this, but...

He lifts her up again. There is no weight at all. He holds her like she's a toddler before setting her back on the divan.

Adrenalin courses in him.

We will feast, he declares. And you will be my honoured guest, Prince Ismael Ben Haddaj. He flourishes a hand through the air. And... Yes. We will announce a betrothal. If you agree, of course. He nods towards Ben Haddaj. I'm sure you will agree — my daughter is beautiful. You will adore Zoraida.

Alaman strides out of the room, ordering food for Casilda, beckoning Ben Haddaj to follow.

Sundown

April 2019

We have to see Eliška for Passover, Casilda insists.

You've been very ill, Miriam says. We don't have to rush. And when did you last keep Passover?

Casilda's room, now their shared room, is full of flowers. Today a large bouquet of peonies has arrived.

From Isak, Casilda tells her, smiling. The note with them says 'This year in Prague.'

So Eliška and Iask really are…?

Looks that way. Casilda is radiant. And chocolates as well. She points to a large red box on the bed. So you were right about them and we need to be there.

In that case, yes.

Miriam knows that Casilda won't approve, but she mentions the concert anyway.

Please tell me you're not serious. It's not even music, just noise.

Mystic Caravan, for goodness sake! So derivative. It was done in the Sixties by Quicksilver. And much better. Have I taught you nothing? Oh, God—unbearable! Casilda falls back on her pillow, dramatically, but she is laughing. She eats a third chocolate. I'm feeling rather queasy now.

Miriam laughs. Mystic Caravan are not that bad. And we need to get out of the house more, especially if we're really going to Prague for Passover. And anyway, I thought you liked La Casa de las Musas.

Casilda shrugs. I like it when I'm performing there. It's a good venue for real music.

Snob, Miriam says, but laughs. I'll play you Diamonds in the Mud on Bandcamp later. You might love it after all.

Later, Miriam puts on *Luna Sefardita* at high volume, filling the house

Now that's music. Casilda grins as she enters the kitchen. She's dressed in a long blue skirt and embroidered blouse and her hair is washed, wild curls tumbling around her face.

So when is this concert at La Casa de las Musas? Casilda asks between forkfuls of tomato and morcilla.

Thursday.

And we go to Prague?

Next Tuesday. We'll have a day to get over the travelling and then we'll help Eliška shop and cook for Passover.

Isak can do that, Casilda says and grins. Who would have guessed?

Me.

Clever clogs. Okay, I'll give it a try, the concert I mean. And… when we get home… get back here… I need to think about what to do with this place.

You won't keep it?

I'm not sure. The dance studio I'm fine about selling. This place has more emotional pull, but I'd really like to be in Toledo. And…

Miriam reaches out and rests a hand on Casilda's arm.

And I'm not sure I want the constant reminders… but… I don't know how I'd feel about letting it go, either.

Maybe it will be easier to think about when you're not here, Miriam suggests.

Yes. Yes, perhaps. But it's not just my decision… I mean — we need to settle somewhere. We have to find a place where both of us can be at home.

Yes, Miriam agrees. It's about time we were always coming home.

Crossing Over
Miriam Catherine McManus

Chapter 4

He clutches his stomach as the last wrenching stream of vomit falls into the basin.

He wants to see Casilda, alone, but it is not possible. He is betrothed to Zoraida. He cannot wander through the Alcázar to the room of a young princess, even one who spends hours each day learning from the doctors and mathematicians her father has attracted to Toledo. He's loitered in the gardens for the last few days, joining in the conversations between Casilda and Ibn Wâfid or Abd' Walid al-Waqqal.

Alchemy is not about gold, Ibn Wâfid says, agreeing with something Casilda has just said, which Ben Haddaj has already forgotten, too busy looking into her green eyes, worrying about the grey shadows around them. The real alchemy is to find medicines, Ibn Wâfid finishes.

But the real problem is not in the body, Casilda responds. Her voice sounds distant. The body is a reasonable animal, it knows what is needed.

She speaks so quietly that all three men lean towards her and Ben Haddaj notices Sulema take a protective step closer.

It's not material that is the problem and not mind either,

not quite, Casilda continues, but something deeper, the problem and the cure are so deep within. Somehow we have to make harmony between all the elements we are made of.

Ibn Wâfid and Abd' Walid al-Waqqal nod vigorously.

There are many stages, princess, Abd' Walid al-Waqqal says. We are constantly destroyed and remade along the way in order to be transformed.

The problem is how to go on in the world, Casilda says. She looks at him directly. Do you agree, Prince Ben Haddaj?

She looks paler each day, Ben Haddaj thinks. The circles around her eyes have darkened even while they've been sat in the garden. He is certain the bleeding must have begun again, but Ahmed has told him that his stubborn little sister insists that she needs nothing, will not allow even Ibn Wâfid to prescribe her simples.

Ben Haddaj pauses. I think perhaps the only way is to become the healing, Princess Casilda.

She smiles. Yes, a higher life is a simple life. The heart becomes peaceful. But we will go through many dark clouds first.

He keeps hearing those words: *we will go through many dark clouds first*. He imagines that, after the ghastly extravagance of the betrothal banquet he's endured this evening, he will no longer be able to join Casilda even in the gardens; not even chaperoned by her eminent tutors and the ever-watchful Sulema. No doubt any contact will be deemed inappropriate. Will he ever be able to speak to her alone again? *We will go through many dark clouds first*.

He pours water into a basin and splashes his face. He pours more into a tall glass and gulps, the bile still burning his throat. He would like to walk, but it is dark and he is uncertain how wandering the corridors or gardens at night would be interpreted.

You are very restless, he hears Casilda say.

He turns and she is there, though there has been no sound or hint of movement.

How...?

She smiles. As it says in Surat Azamar Ayah 42, in dreams the soul departs the body and returns with the permission of Allah.

And we may meet other souls in dreams, he responds, but I'm not asleep, princess... This is more than... Is this what you do when you visit the prisoners?

She shakes her head. I go in body. I have bread to carry.

Of course. Or roses. Ibn Sina believes miracles happen when the inner desire has an outer effect. You are an alchemist already?

I'm not sure what I am, but...

Me neither, he interrupts, but I know I lo...

Shh. This isn't our time. You have your quest.

To marry your sister?

No. You know that won't happen. You don't need me to tell you that.

So I'll tell them I must first make a pilgrimage and...

And they will think you intend to travel to Mecca, not to Jerusalem.

And then?

She shakes her head. It's not always good to see too far ahead.

We will go through many dark clouds first?

She tilts her head, a rueful smile and perhaps the hint of a tear.

I had to come to Toledo, he says.

I know. And I'm grateful for it. You've given me enough health to travel to Burgos.

And you will be healed there?

She pauses long enough for him to taste bile rising again.

Casilda?

For a little while, she says.

And we can't change this? We're just puppets?

No, we're not. I don't believe that. But sometimes...

She steps closer to him and he puts out a hand towards her, thinking to meet only air, gasps.

You're... How can you be here?

I am sleeping peacefully in my bed, she says, her smile

widening. And yet... She shrugs. But to answer your question — it is not fate keeping us apart, it is something in each of us. We have too much to learn to be together in this life, but one day... when our hearts have become peaceful...

You think the Tawhid, the Returning, involves more than one earthly life?

I think what we believe might not be the most important thing.

And what is the most important?

Perhaps what we do, how we live.

And how will you live in Burgos?

Very simply. No more silks and palaces. I'll follow the captives'saviour for a while and learn something of healing and peace. What matters is what's within. I'll miss my conversations with the great thinkers my father has brought to Toledo, but I have a quest.

But... He closes his eyes for a moment, trying to summon the words that might convince her there is a another way and, when he opens them, she is gone.

A Tree Too Weak to Stand

December 2019

What really happened was that I was slow to learn. Belief may have been my gift, but it took me lifetimes to believe that I could find and keep love.

Miriam waits in the green room, a radio interview in the lead-up to her novella coming out.

She clasps a proof of the book, gazes at the cover: Crossing Over, a novella by Miriam McManus. She does not need any other identity. If she was once Casilda and Miriam was once Ben Haddaj, now they are finally the people who will end this story:

Miriam Catherine McManus and Casilda Selene Feartes. It is all we need to be. The story and the facts finally match, she thinks.

There was an incident so slight, so small, that she could not go on.

He's been in her dreams since she was twelve years old. The beach goes on forever… They're chatting about the weather… He puts an arm around her shoulder… There is a movement so small, so strange, something in the way he tucks her into his thin frame… No, she shouts. No. She pulls away.

For pity's sake, Simon, what are you saying? She is not Catherine.

I know that. Of course I do. I didn't mean I'd… It's just… Oh, God, Eliška…

…She's… sensitive.

Like Catherine.

Like, yes… but…

But she is …

God always demands a sacrifice, Casilda.

December 6 is a Friday this year.

We're ready for you, Ms McManus.

An intern hovers by her chair. She looks up, confused.

Sorry, I was miles away.

Once there was a Moorish princess, Casilda… she reads from the novella as the interview ends.

She phones Casilda as soon as she's out of the building.

Miri, are you okay? You sound...

I'm fine. The interview was fine, it's just...

December 6?

Yes.

A bad day for both of us.

Of course, I wasn't even thinking... I...

I wish I was there with you.

Me too.

But you'll be okay?

Of course. She means it at last.

Simon was a good dad, wasn't he?

Yes, he was. Yes.

Go and toast him then.

Do you remember any of it? Miriam asks.

Any of what?

Being Simon, being Ben Haddaj. I mean... Simon had dreams of Ben Haddaj's death and Catherine dreamt your grandmother's life and sensed Casilda when she visited Toledo. I don't seem to... to feel the same except in rare strange moments. I think I felt it more when I was a child, but now...

I felt it the day Simon died, Casilda says softly. But now... no, not so much. I was thinking about it this morning actually, and I suddenly thought, no, not so much thought... it was almost like I heard you saying it: Miriam Catherine McManus and Casilda Selene Faertes. It is all we need to be. The story and the facts finally match.

What?

Just something that popped into my mind this morning, but it was like you'd said it to me.

Miriam's voice quavers. That's exactly what I thought while I was waiting for the interview.

There is a pause.

Wow, that's... Casilda laughs. Actually, maybe that's par for the course.

There is another pause.

Maybe the others, the people we've been... they weren't ready... or... Casilda's voice trails away.

A tree too weak to stand, Miriam says.

Yes, Casilda agrees. But now...

In the hotel room, Miriam puts the proof beside her bed, opens a bottle of sparkling water from the mini fridge and toasts Simon.

There was an incident so slight, so small, and now it's gone. She raises her glass. Thank you, she says. Thank you, Dad. I love you.

In the shower she pictures a night in December when she sat on her bedroom floor, shivering. Her clothes stuck to her, rain-sodden, icy. She couldn't remember leaving the house on a wet December night, walking into the darkness; rain and wind harrying her. She knew only that she'd had to get outside, to cry for Simon in the obliterating Welsh rain.

It's okay, Miriam, Eliška reassured. We'll be okay. Come and get into the bath, it's all poured. I'll make you hot chocolate and you can sleep. We'll talk more tomorrow. We'll talk as much as you want. We can do this, Miriam.

She remembers hot water in the deep bath, bath oil scented with lavender and geranium. Sinking into the scent and steam, she'd repeated the mantra that Simon had told her Catherine often used: all shall be well and all shall be well and all manner of thing shall be well… All shall be well. We can do this, she'd said aloud, sinking deeper into fragrant water.

She orders hot chocolate from the room service number. You do know there's a £4 tray charge, the young man on the other end enquires. Maybe you'd like something else with it?

Just the chocolate, she says in Czech, picking up his accent. I'm toasting my father with it. I'll stand the £4.

Of course, he says, flustered. Of course.

She picks up one of Catherine's journals that she has carried with her.

The next day in Nice, I visited the Chagall museum. I sat in front of 'Moses with the Burning Bush', felt myself falling:

...numinous burning, red and yellow against blue-blue-blue. Moses on his knees, transfigured — and I am transformed with him — the power of being: I will be who I will be. Raw energy. To be, to be new, to go on being, not to expire — to have a future — burning, always, not consumed. I was. I am. I will be. Will I?

I'd brushed away a stray tear, moved on to 'Noah's Ark':

...blue-blue waters rising, a bird here, goat there. And the people, waiting in the wings of apocalypse, huddled. Who will make it? There are mothers holding children, families clustered, a man on his knees, behind him a woman stands, head bent to his, arms wrapping him. Will they make it?

How many can an Ark hold? And the covenant, what is that? The rainbow promise of no more destruction? No-one can make that promise, not even God, I thought, remembering a time when I believed, a time before I lost my baby, that savage flow of blood.

A woman across the gallery glanced at me as though she could hear my thoughts. Did she remind me of Miriam or was that only my muddled mind?

Again and again, the earth is wiped out. Tribulation. A people who are persecuted, and now? I tried to think of what Miriam would say about the images; whether the story and the facts would match.

...blue tribulation. Jacob meets the love of his life at the well and how does that go? Fourteen years before they are together. And his beloved child, his son—all that love come to tears, blood, betrayal, loss. And in the middle of this Jacob meets what? Who? Does he fight the ground of being for a place to stand? Jacob—violet on blue, struggling, fighting, changed—

I conjured our first meeting — Your real name is... It took me years to realise that Miriam loved me. Yet, despite that love, even Miriam could see only the Cassie she had made up or wanted me to be: Casilda. I believed all of it and none of it. And now? The Chagall haunted me:

...so we fight with being itself to discover who we are; limp on, walking out of a past of victories and defeats and into a future of unimagined losses, fears and hopes; wounded and blessed.

In the room of *Le Cantique des Cantiques* the canvasses were red.

I started to weep, clutching my stomach.

Madame? The attendant reached out a hand tentatively, but pulled it back as I looked up. *Madame? Vous êtes...*

I could only shake my head. I'm fine, I managed at last. It's just the pictures... they're very moving.

The attendant nodded, moved away, glancing back at me.

I noticed the woman, who was so like Miriam, same olive skin, same pitch-dark hair, hovering nearby. I think I smiled at her. Catherine, I said.

Miriam, she replied.

I startled at that and noticed her gaze fall on my hand of Miriam pendant.

I had a friend called Miriam, I offered, but she died. This hand of Miriam was a gift from her.

My grandmother had one, she said in return. She died two days ago. I'm here to visit her grave.

I nodded. I used to believe, I said, wondering why I was saying so much to a stranger, but going on anyway. Before I lost Miriam, lost my baby, but now...

She nodded. I don't think I've ever believed, not in a traditional sense, and yet...

The world is a strange place, I finished for her.

There's a knock on the hotel-room door.

Your hot chocolate, Ms McManus, a man a little older than me says in Czech.

Thank you! The cup is beautiful, large. On the tray is a dried blue flower, no doubt lifted from one of the hotel arrangements. Thank you!

I snuggle into bed with the chocolate and the journal. Thank you, Simon. Thank you, Catherine. Thank you Eliška. Thank you Miriam. To all of you! I raise my chocolate and sip.

Crossing Over
Miriam Catherine McManus

Chapter 5

Is there nothing I can say to convince you to stay in Burgos, Princess Casilda? We can have water brought from the well at San Vicente. You don't need to make such a difficult journey.

Casilda smiles and shakes her head. Thank you, but it's not only to visit the well... I'm planning to live there.

In the hills? There are villages close by, but they're not what you're used to... And at this time of year there's likely to be snow. At least stay with us until spring...

Thank you, but you don't need to worry about me. I'm sure Sulema would prefer to stay here though and I'd be grateful if you could arrange her safe journey back to Toledo.

Sulema glances anxiously at Muniadona, wife of Sancho the Great. I must go with my princess, Sulema says stiffly.

As you both wish. Of course, we'll arrange for you to be accompanied to Briviesca. And I'll make sure you have food and...

Casilda shakes her head again. Thank you, but we will be provided for along the way, and the snow won't touch us.

Muniadona smiles. The letter from your father warned me that you have a strong will. Strong enough that he sent you here and asked me to ensure you get to the holy well in whatever way you request.

Thank you.

But you will rest here tonight?

We would be glad to. You're very kind.

On her way to her room in the palace, she first climbs the tower overlooking the gate at the north of the castle. From the top she can see out across the plains. Huddled around the castle are many dwellings, fires flickering in the dusk. To the north-east, far beyond sight, is Briviesca and, beyond that, the holy well. She leans toward it, breathing in the early evening air.

That night she dreams of a ship — fifty or sixty feet end to end — one mast, one square sail fronting the enormous waves. She hears a voice reciting a strange litany: *myrrh, pepper, cinnamon, saffron, cardamom, silk... myrrh, pepper, cinnamon, saffron...* as though the words are a charm to ward off the sea. She sees Ben Haddaj sitting on a narrow bunk, afraid, yet calm. *Myrrh, pepper, cinnamon, saffron, cardamom, silk.* And then the chant changes—*Shir hama-alos... Out of the depths I call to You, O Lord...*

He walks onto the deck where men are running, trying to steer against the wind with only one unbiddable sail. Ben Haddaj looks up. He can hear sailors cursing the winds, the crew shouting about the changes from westerly to north-westerlies to southerly to violent north-easterly, hollering about how it is sending them off-course and into the pull of waves, swelling and swelling.

Out of the depths I call to You, O Lord...

A wave breaks over their heads and the ship dips as another wave crashes and...

Hear, O Israel! The LORD is our God, the LORD is one! You shall love the LORD your God with all your heart and with all your soul and with all your might...

The next wave batters the men into the deck... and another... and a crack louder than thunder... There is only sea and the cold is so intense, yet she feels he is calm. But when he inhales, water fills him and his body begins to fight. He panics at last, exhaling water, inhaling water so that his lungs burn, his insides tearing, on fire...

Out of the depths I call to You...

And then the peace deepens, there is only tranquillity... *out of the depths...* such serenity... and he surrenders...

She wakes sobbing, pushing the blankets from her face, disoriented... Sulema is at her side, distraught, but trying to comfort her.

It's just a dream, my angel. Shh, shh. I'll fetch some water.

She sits up, gulping down tears. He's gone, Sulema. In this life...

Who? Who's gone? You were only dreaming. It was...

Casilda puts a hand on Sulema's arm. No, it was true. Ben Haddaj drowned on his way to Jerusalem. One day we will be together, our hearts will be at peace, but first we will go through many dark clouds.

Sulema puts a hand on Casilda's forehead. You are feverish, she says. I'll fetch that water. But when she returns with the glass she adds, Allah have mercy on his soul. He was a good man.

Race Among the Ruins

December 2007

I didn't see anyone but Eliška for months. When we arrived in Prague, she gave me her beautiful bedroom, filled it with books, bought me a CD player and a laptop and let me work out how to spend my days. I went to bed, stayed there day after day, week after week, months lost in dreams or in memories I might have invented.

In the house that Catherine had made her sanctuary in Wales after she was divorced from Liam, I would take refuge under the table, cocooned with hand-coloured paper dolls on wooden skewers, acting out stories I'd write in my head, crouched with the fantasies no-one else could enter. The wood-burner would slowly spread its warmth through the kitchen. Sometimes Simon would ask me about the stories, but he never suggested changes or told me to go out and play with the children kicking balls in the spring rain or sledding down the road at the other side of the house in winter.

You'll be a great writer, like your mum, he would say.

Actor, I'd shoot back. I'm going to be an actor.

Of course. A writer and an actor.

Outside, enormous skies, the scents of coal-smoke and damp, the hiss of the river running along the garden. When the children who played in the cul-de-sac had gone home to bed, I'd stand in the garden, drinking in a place that had been my mother's, longing for memory. It made me sensitive to the appeal of daydreams, to stories in which there was always an absent mother.

At school I stood by the fence. A boy sauntered across the yard, leant down, asked, are you okay?

I looked at him, puzzled.

I'm Ifan, he said. Are the other kids leaving you out? Then he added, Do you speak Welsh?

Dw'in siarad Cymraeg, I told him. I'm watching them. I'm making them up.

He looked at me, still puzzled. You don't want to play?

I am playing, I told him. I'm playing 'they're my story'.

He shrugged. You shout me if they give you any trouble. All right, Cyw?

Miriam, I corrected. Not a chick. I'm called Miriam.

He grinned and sauntered away. Ta'ra, Miriam Cyw.

When I was six we moved to live by the sea. The sky was simple; a light-blue crystal. It may be fragile like me, I thought. I walked through marram grass, through dry cutting sand, buff damp sand. The dunes hid a fat triangle of glass that pierced between my toes. Simon came running at my cry and carried me home to the house looking out across Harlech. The blood, redder than the dragon waving on the flag, oozed viscous. I felt strange; the sky sun-spattered, blue-vulnerable. My imaginary mother walked with us. Nearly there, Catherine said, stroking my hair; foot throbbing, sand sticking to the blood.

Nearly home, Simon said.

In the kitchen, he sat me on the table we'd brought from Catherine's cottage, cleaned away the sand carefully, pressed hard to stop the blood, stuck a plaster over the mess. I didn't know until that day that I was allergic to sticking-plaster.

I'll make sandwiches, Simon said, hugging me.

Memory, always made of objects: the oiled wood of the table, photos of Catherine, pictures of herself as a baby. In all of them, the paper dolls, their edges curling. No ideas but in things, Simon would say, but some things were more amorphous: the soothing scents of wood burning in the stove and rain on the salt-air, the sharp odour of oranges that made her stomach turn to acid pain. The hardback copy of *Casilda of the Rising Moon* that had been her mother's, that Simon gave her for her tenth birthday.

Casilda. She repeated the word, liking the taste on her tongue, pale and delicate. It's who you really are — this is just an enchantment, my darling girl, her imaginary mother told her.

Who am I?

She wakes in the night, sits up in bed, asks the darkness, Who am I?

Miriam? Miriam, I'm here. Eliška is by her side. Go to sleep, sweetheart. I'm here. Eliška tucks the blankets around her.

No. She sits up.

Was it a dream? Eliška sits by her on the bed.

I don't remember, only... I suddenly didn't know who I was... I thought I was...

What?

I don't know. I heard someone say... *It's who you really are—this is just an enchantment, my darling girl.* I've heard that before, but I can't remember where... And then a voice said, *Remember, the story and the facts must match.*

She watches Eliška shiver.

Do you know?

It sounds like Catherine, Eliška whispers.

I think she's with me sometimes. I used to... when I was little... she was like my imaginary friend, but not imaginary, not outside me either, something inside... I haven't felt that for ages, though, not since... since Simon gave me her book. When I was ten. Miriam springs from the bed to fetch the hardback of *Casilda of the Rising Moon*. She waves it at Eliška. That's when I heard those words before. When Simon gave me this...

She trails away, begins to cry. Eliška moves to her side and holds her tightly.

I don't feel him, Eliška. I never feel Simon is still... He's just gone... completely gone...

Long into the night, after Eliška has soothed her and tucked her up like a baby, she lies awake, drifts towards a half sleep, into the images of dreams, where...

She is by the sea. The sky is simple; a light-blue crystal. It may be fragile like me, she thinks.

The beach goes on forever, a boundary of coarse sand and marram grass further from the tide line... She is walking with Simon, Eliška ahead of them in the distance. They walk where the sand is wet, the shuck of bare feet on grains moist with salt and sea. Miriam watches the footprints, Simon's prints are long and thin. She is dressed in a creamy-white tunic, transparent cheesecloth floating from her thin torso on breaths of sea breeze, over a white cotton skirt edged in broderie anglaise.

She puts on her sandals as they reach the marram grass, walking through dry cutting sand, remembering the fat triangle of glass that pierced between her toes not long after they moved to Harlech. They are talking about Eliška and Uncle Nathan, how they might split up... he winds his arm around her as they walk...

No, Miriam shouts. No!

She runs, calling out to Eliška...

God always demands sacrifice.

She is the ram caught in the thicket on a beach

She feels sand sticking to blood.

The story and the facts don't match...

She wakes filmed in sour milk sweat.

She sits up in bed, turns on the light, reaches for the journal that she hasn't written in since Simon died. Writes:

Until death, it's all life, Miriam. Remember.

Yes, she says out loud to the night.

The unreason of the world is more insane than any fiction.

The clock says 5 a.m. She turns off the light, pulls the blanket close, certain she won't get back to sleep, where...

There is a scent of oranges, a pulse of music, insistent.

A girl of about sixteen smiles at her. She has olive skin, hair a tangle of soot and pitch.

I brought your cure when you were weak, almost dead, Casilda, the girl is saying, the talisman that would bring your cure, knowing that you had secretly given your heart to the Christian saviour, risking your father's wrath. I made a vow then that if the relic cured you, if you lived, I would return to the religion of my fathers, to the God of Abraham, Isaac and Jacob. When I arrived in Toledo your father was beyond himself with grief. I had a hard time persuading King Alamun to allow me even one minute alone with you and your nurse. You were so pale that, for a moment, I thought I'd arrived too late, but your eyes flickered and you told me you had been expecting me. I had brought you a scrap of the Virgin's robe, dipped in holy water, and I knew that if you had found faith you would live. You said simply, I believe, and were well again. It wasn't the relic of course, it wasn't magic that healed you, but faith. Belief is your gift. I believe, you said, and then you were laughing and well and Alamun and his men were in the room, swords drawn, amazed to see you sitting up, healthy and happy.

I knew the price of saving you would be terrible. That I would be betrothed to your sister Zoraida as a reward, that I could not refuse the powerful Alamun and his son Ahmed, my allies. I was like Abraham commanded to kill his son. I had been commanded to put aside my love for you in order to save you, Casilda.

The girl drops her voice to a whisper. God always demands a sacrifice, Casilda, even after saying he's through with it.

She wakes with an ache low in her abdomen. The feeling of... She fingers the sticky mess.

In the shower, she watches blood circle the drain, tang of iron on the tongue. It's still early and the bathroom is cold. She steps onto the cool cream tiles of the bathroom, wet, shaking, still bleeding. She makes a pad from a flannel and wraps her thin body in an old towel.

Miriam?

Sorry, I didn't mean to wake you again. I got my period...

Oh, sweetheart. Eliška pulls her close. Get into bed. I'll make you some mint tea., maybe some chamomile in it too?

Miriam curls into a ball, fingers the little hand of Miriam that hangs on a silk cord around her neck. When she wakes the mint tea is cooling on the table beside her.

What really happened was that I didn't see anyone but Eliška for months.

But after my first period started, I got up next morning and wanted to explore Prague. I knew I had to find the girl with olive skin, hair a tangle of soot and pitch... whoever she was. I had to find her because somehow she would lead me back to... I wasn't sure what she would lead me back to, only that I no longer felt Simon had completely left me...

Crossing Over
Miriam Catherine McManus

Chapter 6

I have one more request, Casilda tells Muniadona the next day. Before we leave for Briviesca, and on to Bureba, I wish to be baptised.

Sulema sucks in air loudly, but says nothing, looking from her princess to Muniadona, eyes wide with questions she cannot ask.

And you Sulema? Muniadona asks.

Sulema shakes her head. Allah preserve us all, she says.

Muniadona smiles. We could use the waters of San Vicente if you would prefer, Casilda. I can send for them. Then perhaps you might rethink your journey?

Casilda smiles but shakes her head. The water of Burgos will suffice. Last night I dreamt of water taking someone I loved from the world, at least for a little time. Today the waters of baptism will take me to a new beginning.

Muniadona nods. I will make the arrangements.

When they set out towards the plains and mountains of Salinillas de Bureba the next morning, Sulema argues only a little about going on foot, the two of them alone without a caravan of helpers. She argues more vociferously about leaving behind the pack horse that has been loaded with food, but eventually sighs and throws her hands in the air. As you wish, she says.

Thank you, Sulema, though you really don't need to do this journey. Zoraida would be glad to see you home again. She will have a wedding to prepare for soon.

But you said Ben Haddaj...

Ben Haddaj was never going to be Zoraida's husband, but in a little time she will meet the man who will be her first husband.

The first?

Zoraida will marry a noble ally of my father's and have beautiful children, but his kingdom will fail and she will have to flee. But another king will love her and one day she'll be baptised in Burgos just as I was.

Baptised? Zoraida? Allah save us!

There are many good years to come for her before then, Sulema. And more good years after that before... But that's a long way off. You should be with her.

I'm not leaving you, Sulema says, adding, Before what, Casilda?

It's not always a blessing to know the future. I shouldn't have said so much.

But you did.

Casilda sighs, but says softly. She will marry a Christian prince and be baptised Isabel. She will have another son, a beautiful boy, but other babies will not live and finally...

There is a long pause before Sulema prompts, Finally?

As the leaves are about to fall at the turn to September...
It will be like my mother, Sulema, and still so young...

In childbirth?

Casilda nods.

Sulema hugs her tight. You are right. It's a curse to know too much. I shouldn't have pressed.

Will you return to her now?

My place is with you.

As you wish. Casilda hugs her in return. So we should make a start.

As they set out, an anxious-looking Muniadona watches them leave.

They walk in silence for several miles before Sulema ventures, Is everything we do already written for us?

We carry our fates in our souls, Sulema, Casilda tells her. It's ours to make. Our dreams will show us the right direction.

I'm afraid I don't really understand, Sulema says quietly. I'm not going to be much use for you to talk to, am I? There's no Ibn Wâfid for all those clever discussions now, just an old woman who has no idea what all this is about. I only hope your sister will know happiness along the way and I hope your dreams will show us where to find food.

The path will be full of kind strangers, Casilda reassures.

And when we get to the cave, we will find fruit and berries and the villagers will bring eggs and milk.

The cave?

It will be dry and safe and we will make it cosy. Other kinds of humans lived there a million years ago.

Other kinds of humans?

There were many, Sulema. They didn't survive the ages, but they left echoes in the mountains and one day we will know more about them. But that is long into the future.

Sulema opens her mouth, but closes it again. They walk in silence until the snow begins to fall.

Oh, Casilda, we have to go back. This is...

Sulema falls quiet, gazing at Casilda, who appears to be walking in a pool of light. Come close, the girl whispers. Keep warm, Sulema.

It is only by the soreness of her feet and her thirst that Sulema knows she has walked all day. They have hardly spoken and the winter sun is sinking.

There's a hamlet at the foot of Mount Pelado, Casilda tells her. One day it will have a hostel and many pilgrims will walk this way, but today we will find a family ready to give us a place to sleep.

Sulema is too weary to reply or to argue when Casilda knocks on the door of a poor looking house built of roof stone. The child who answers looks half-starved and sickly, but Casilda greets the girl by name and asks about her mother, Adelita.

When they have eaten and both the child and Casilda have settled to sleep, Adelita pours barley tea into two bowls and hands one to Sulema.

My kitchen was almost bare when you knocked, Adelita says. Yet when I came to cook there were not only lentils, but fresh leeks and an eggplant, olive oil, eggs and bread that I didn't have this morning. And Gota hasn't coughed all evening. I haven't seen her looking so well since she was a toddler.

Sulema smiles and shrugs. I don't know what to tell you, she says. I've walked through snow today. I'm bone-tired, but I didn't even feel the cold while I was walking next to her.

Is she an angel?

She's a very sick young woman and yet... even though I wish she was at home, a princess in a palace, she seems, like Gota, to be healthier than I've seen her since she was a little girl. And nothing will turn her back from going to the springs. She learnt about them from prisoners in her father's dungeon and is determined to live there.

A noise makes the women pause. A fall?

Sulema nods and rises. In the tiny room separated from the main living area by a thin door of gnarled planks is a small bed. Gota is asleep, but Casilda is on the floor, kneeling and doubled over, rocking. Sulema springs towards her, but cannot move the small body or make contact with Casilda, who seems to be in a trance, far away. Adelita moves towards them to help and together they lay Casilda next to the sleeping child, her eyes wide open, but vacant, her skin cold.

Don't cry, Sulema. The voice is small and seems to come

from another world, but Casilda blinks and smiles. *I was travelling. Don't worry about me. I'm in no danger here.*

Oh, Casilda. Sulema chokes back the guttural tears, hoping not to wake the child, but Gota merely stirs and turns in her sleep. I thought... Sulema sniffs hard and Adelita lays a hand on her arm.

I will be well soon, Sulema. When I reach the white springs, I'll bathe in the water to finish the healing Ben Haddaj began. And then I'll stay and help others who come to the springs. I'll make a bed in the cave and drink the water and eat berries. But I must be alone, Sulema. Zoraida needs you at home and I have to make this journey by myself.

But I... You can't... How can I leave you? I've been with you since your poor mother... I took you from her arms before she... Oh, Casilda.

Casilda stands shakily and leads Sulema back into the main room of the cottage, Adelita following.

You don't need to worry about me, Casilda insists when they are seated around the table again. *I have a long road ahead, but I have seen so many wonderful things in my dreams. I will...* She pauses. *We will go through many dark clouds first, but in the end... hope is always born at the same time as love.*

I don't understand...

I know it's hard. But promise me you will return to Zoraida. Please promise.

I can't imagine a day without you in it, Sulema says, but I can't imagine going against your implacable will, either.

Thank you, Sulema. Tomorrow, one of Adelita's neighbours is making a journey and will take you back to Burgos. This time with a pony. And you will be safely taken from there to Toledo. Now I must sleep. I have my own journey tomorrow, to Briviesca and then to Salinillas de Bureba, up into the hills.

But how you will live there? You can't really live alone in a cave?

It's a good cave, right by the springs. It housed a mother bear and three cubs last winter and will be safe and snug.

A bear's cave? But they'll come back. They might already be there.

No, the cave is empty this year, it's waiting for me.

Sulema purses her lips and shakes her head. But you'll be so lonely.

I'll be alone, but not lonely, Casilda replies. I have to be alone to empty myself, Sulema, and then I will be filled with hope and love.

Changes

October 2010

What really happened was that I started to recover from the grief after that first period. Eliška had given me a whole year to hide away and I was ready to face the world again. But I refused to go to school, even after I had stopped grieving alone in my room. I sensed there was more to the world than I could learn in a classroom.

You'd learn Czech much more quickly in school, Eliška reasoned, but I was already learning the language and we spoke in Czech at home more and more. And you'd make friends, she added.

I can make friends at a homeschool group, I countered.

Eliška wrinkled her nose. They're all ex-pat Americans, she said.

Don't be a snob, I replied, laughing. Anyway, lots of your friends are American.

We'll give it a try. You know you still have to register with a school that allows you to learn at home, don't you? And some nosy inspector will come poking around twice a year, so you'd better keep up with all your subjects.

I threw my arms round her. I will, I promised. Can you teach me Spanish?

Spanish?

I want to read more about Casilda and most of the documents are in Spanish.

She sighed theatrically, but said, Of course I can, but you're on your own with maths. Okay?

It's a deal.

What really happened was that I hardly ever joined in with any of the organised groups for homeschoolers. I would walk miles around the city each morning, leaving Eliška's flat on Vlašská when she left for work and soaking up the city, notebook in hand, books in Czech and English and Spanish in an old duffel bag that had belonged to Simon. I'd end up at the archive where Eliška worked and where she had helped Simon with the book he was researching before he went to Budapest to be with Catherine. We'd eat sandwiches together and then I'd go back to the flat and study.

We had no problems with the school inspectors, even in maths. My friends were not other teenagers, but Eliška's friends: a gallery owner, Gabriel, who taught me to draw; a woman called Agáta, who wore wildly coloured velvet coats and made marionettes; academics and writers, who treated my growing obsessions with Sufism, alchemy and Kabbalah as serious pursuits.

What really happened was that the nightmares stopped. I retained the sense that Catherine was with me, but gradually it became a background comfort. I remembered Simon and no longer thought of him as utterly lost. But I forgot the girl in my dream who had brought him back to me, the girl with wild dark curls.

I saw the gifts piled on the table when I woke on Sunday 31 October, my sixteenth birthday. The table was Catherine's, we'd taken it from her cottage in the hills in Wales to our seaside kitchen in Harlech and now it was here in Prague. I'd never thought about how much it must have cost Eliška to have it shipped there to take up nearly all of the dining area in her elegant apartment.

Each present was carefully wrapped in tissue paper, lilac and coral, mint and apricot, sage and sapphire. There were plum and poppy seed kolá
 and a cake plate bearing a whole medovnik.

Happy birthday, Eliška greeted me.

I stood still, gazing at the table.

It's… it looks so much.

Well, it's not all from me. Eliška laughed. Even Nathan remembered your sixteenth.

Wow!

Yes. My ex never quite got significant events for the most part.

Can I open them?

You can.

I don't know where to start.

How about with hot chocolate and pastries, then you can sit

and slowly open teach one. Some of them will need a bit of explanation.

Okay.

This is from Gabriel, Eliška tells her when they've cleared the table of crumbs and Eliška has produced two more mugs of steaming, rich chocolate.

Miriam peels the tape from the mint tissue paper and eases out a wooden square that frames a painting of Simon and Catherine.

He worked from a photo, Eliška says.

It's beautiful.

She takes a large breath. The lilac tissue is criss-crossed with velvet ribbon in deep plum. Agáta? Miriam asks.

Eliška nods.

The wooden box inside is about eighteen inches long. Its lid slides off like a huge pencil case to reveal a marionette, an exquisitely delicate princess in a robe of such pale blue it is almost white, like the halo of sky around the sun. She has long golden hair, green eyes, pale skin.

Casilda, Miriam whispers, sniffing back a tear.

Eliška reaches out a hand and strokes her hair.

Miriam smiles. People are so kind… She takes a deep breath. Can I open the tiny one?

Beneath the sapphire wrapping is a tiny cardboard box

decorated with stylised brown leaves and flowers. Inside, purple tissue paper cradles a silver pendant, a tulip with a row of diminutive garnets trailing from its fine stem.

It's gorgeous, Miriam says, holding it to the light so that the garnets fill with deep red.

It was Catherine's. Simon gave it to her in Budapest, but he bought it here in Prague. It was his idea of an engagement ring.

Oh! Miriam's tears flow this time, but she wipes a hand across her face and smiles. I'm not... I mean... I'm so happy... it's just...

I know, darling. I know. Do you want a break?

No, no I'm fine. She takes a long gulp of chocolate. Which one next?

How about Nathan's? Eliška hands her the book-shaped sage parcel.

Inside is a pristine hardback in a plastic wrapping: *In a Place of Transformation and Dread*, a novel by Simon Garrett.

I know you have a copy, but this is the only proof copy we know of, Eliška tells her.

Miriam takes it out of the wrapping as though it might disintegrate. It's wonderful, she says, but Nathan — won't he miss it?

It was his idea. He says he's been waiting for the right time...

It's wonderful, Miriam repeats.

There are several sheets of coral tissue around the largest gift on the table and Miriam stands to peel it away, revealing a huge cardboard box filled with journals. She looks up at Eliška, who nods. Catherine's, Eliška says. But try not to read them all at once. Will you be okay with them? If you'd rather not…

They're so lovely, Miriam says, fingering a book made of pale wood with a spine of soft indigo suede, lifting out another with a tooled leather device of hares on the front and another covered in jewel-bright emerald silk.

They are beautiful, Eliška agrees. Last one?

Miriam places a marbled-covered journal back into the box and reaches for the last gift, a slim rectangle covered in apricot tissue and gold satin ribbon.

It's not quite so exotic, Eliška says apologetically, but hopefully useful.

A pen?

Open it and see.

It's… Oh, but Eliška, it's… it's too much… I…

I'm not expecting you to spend it all. I've been putting money in since… goodness… since you were a baby, but more since you came to live with me. It will help with your education. I have a feeling you'll want to travel as well, in time. So it's for those things—the big things that…

Miriam throws her arms round her aunt, sobbing. Thank you, she manages at last. And I won't waste it. Thank you!

Crossing Over
Miriam Catherine McManus

Chapter 7

Emerging from the spring on a bitter November day, Casilda feels only warmth. The blood stopped the instant she stepped into the crystal water. She feels hunger for the first time in... she can hardly remember. In the cave behind her is a basket of cheese and fruit, a pitcher of goat's milk, a loaf of rye bread.

She brings the food to a flat stone at the mouth of the cave. There is a smattering of snow on the ground and her rough, undyed cloak is not a thick weave, but an inner warmth sustains her. She eats and drinks slowly, relishing each mouthful and watching a young female mountain lion hunting rabbits in the dawn light. Later the lion, Beatriz, will settle beside her on the flat stone, viewing the valley. Casilda stays on the stone, gazing across hills and fields, but she does not see the slopes and trees, only distant worlds. Her vision swims and...

in a world of red...

... she is a child hobbling. The blood, redder than the iron scars on the wet beach, oozing, viscous. She feels faint; the sky sun-spattered, blue-vulnerable. Her imaginary friend, Marina, walks with her to the pole at the end of the beach.

Nearly there, Marina says, encouraging her to hobble the last few yards; foot throbbing, sand sticking to the blood.

Marina, Casilda says to the countryside towards the tiny hamlet of Buezo. The saint the prisoners told me about...

A man wrenches the glass from between her toes, presses hard to stop the blood, sticks a strange pink fabric over the mess.

... a clot slips between her legs, blood thick, gelatinous, oozes through layers of clothing. A man and a woman, young, dressed in the same style of clothes, blue trousers that widen near the ground, bright tunics, wrap a blanket around her and help her into a strange metal contraption on wheels with a slippery seat. She thinks of her Berber mother, haemorrhaging after giving birth to her; of the bleeding that began in the garden as she walked with Zoraida, going on without respite...

...and in an enormous room filled with extraordinary paintings in reds and blues, she hears an inner voice... blue tribulation. Jacob meets the love of his life at the well and how does that go? Fourteen years before they are together. And his beloved child, his son—all that love come to tears, blood, betrayal, loss. And in the middle of this Jacob meets what? Who? Does he fight the ground of being for a place to stand? Jacob—violet on blue, struggling, fighting, changed—

A heavy clot of blood slips between her legs. Unsteady, she glances round. No-one. She huddles into a woollen garment, pulls another around her lower body to hide the blood she feels, oozing through layers of clothing, begins the climb back to the apartment through the steep narrow streets of what is Toledo, but not Toledo as she knows it, cobbles jarring, abdomen aching.

A woman walks beside her.

You fell sick, the woman says. Remember. It was the same illness that your mother died from not long after your birth. There was no way to stop the blood.

She hunches into the pain, feels stickiness seep through thick wool tights. A spasm halts her.

One of the prisoners told you about the wells of San Vicente near Briviesca in la Bureba. And so you persuaded your father to send you there to be healed, became an ascetic like Saint Marina.

Remember the night of your death, how you sent your spirit across Spain to Toledo to be with your father as he passed away. Some stories say you lived to be over a hundred, but we know you died young. Perhaps neither of us stays in a body for long once the other departs.

There is darkness. The world has become black, so thick she can hardly breathe.

She sits on a bench shivering... snow like white sand... She reads *Texts of Terror*, uncertain whether her tears are for Jephthah's daughter or herself... hands close around neck, ragged breath, white cotton tearing... blood, redder than iron on wet beach, oozes, viscous. The sky sun-spattered...

Nearly there, Miriam says.

Sand sticking to blood.

She falls onto sand...

She's not what she seems... another McManus slut...

Yes, Miriam agrees, yes.

Yes... hands around her throat, rough breath, white cotton tearing, blood welling between toes, red skin where the rock hits his thigh...

Run, Cassie, run!

Until death, it's all life, Cassie. Remember.

She enters the yard, walls rising, blind, mute, slabbing out sky, yet its granite light dazzles after the cell's gloom.

She lies wounded among debris, her right arm and leg blood-spattered and fragment-encrusted. She retches from pain, tries to stay conscious, looks round frantically for help.

A voice in the night tells her: Remember, my darling Casilda. Remember, and if you can't remember, invent...

Remember how you studied the Qu'ran from the age of five, how you heard the story of Saint Marina, were fascinated by a king's daughter who ran away to lead a contemplative's life. You learned with the wisest in the taifa, became brilliant, but remained restless, disturbed by the thought of prisoners in the palace dungeons until you took them food, heard their stories, remembered Saint Marina.

What are you carrying?

The soldier accompanying her father blocks her passage down the steps. She shrinks inside the hooded cloak, colour of night sky, lifts the folds of her white silk robe closer, the loaves hidden.

Roses, she says.

She feels a tremor, darkness falls on her before she's hit the ground. When she wakes, the steps beneath are strewn red, the air thick with the scent of roses. Her father holds her in his arms.

She dreams of the Alcázar, its stones shining gold in the last of the evening's sunlight.

Casilda? How?... Have you returned? Sulema will be...

Casilda shakes her head. Sometimes we meet in dreams.

But I wasn't asleep, I... Are you really here? Can I hug you?

You can, Casilda says, and laughs.

You look so well. Golden. You're not nearly so pale and your hair... I wish my hair was golden, Zoraida says.

Your hair is beautiful, she tells her sister. To match your dark eyes and perfect skin. You can have a golden wedding dress made from the silk Ahmed is bringing back with him. It will show off your hair magnificently.

But what about you? Will you be here? Will you wear a golden dress too?

If I wore golden silk I'd look washed out and ill. It's not the colour for me.

You don't need to wear gold, do you? You're an angel. Zoraida pauses. You are an angel, aren't you? Or...

Casilda laughs. Or a demon?

Dreams and alchemy frighten me.

You don't need to worry about me. And as for alchemy, I'm not interested in turning anything into gold, only in transforming myself. The only golden thing I want in my life is a mountain lion called Beatriz who comes to keep me warm at night and tell me about her days.

A lion? But...

Shh, no more worrying. I came to wish you a long life and strong children. Be happy, Zoraida.

There is a blur of yellow mist and Zoraida is alone, a scent of roses hanging in the air.

The world is white, so white.

The snow has almost cleared and yet every surface dazzles. Crystal water bells against rocks, white water and she is in the mosque gardens...

Trees bow under approaching winter, dry leaves shimmer, fall; the large cedar bends to the wind. But where are the fruit trees; the peach, apricot, guava and fig, hunkering against the winter? The fountain by the back wall is empty, but still the sound of water against stone. She whispers a word on the breeze: Tulaytula. And sees a woman turn towards her, as though she has turned to look into a mirror...

The world is white and she is at one with this other woman in another time...

Casilda blinks and shivers. The sun has gone down. The food basket is empty beside her in the shadows. When she stands, she feels the blood sticking to her, sees blood congealing on the rock where she has been sitting for hours while the world turned red, black, gold and white, the tang of iron on her tongue, the water of the spring singing to itself in the growing dark.

She makes her way into the cave, strips away the bloodied robe and wraps herself in a rough blanket, falling asleep curled against the pain. When she wakes, the cave is pitch and she can hear Beatriz's gentle breath, feel the mountain lion's heat next to her. She moves to the entrance where sharp stars dazzle through the darkness. On the flat stone, a tiny fragment catches in a glint of moonlight; a pale silk cord strung with a tiny hand of Fatima in black, silver, gold. Beside it, a turquoise glass of mint tea has cooled.

Never too Close

September 2016

This is what really happened. I came to Toledo in search of Casilda—and to stay close to Catherine... I came to Toledo to be with my mother and the saint she might once have been, and to write. But Casilda was as elusive as reality and my mother had become silent too. Ben Haddaj, if he ever existed, had fallen out of history. He seemed to have lived only in the pages of a worn children's novel that was once my mother's, that I carried with me.

Toledo resonated to a Moorish past—the tiles on the walls, the dishes in the tabernas, the curved swords displayed in shops, the shape of keyhole archways, the Arabic designs on the intricate damascene jewellery of oxidised black steel inlaid with filigree silver and gold, adorning every other shop window. Yet little of the eleventh century could be touched: stones in the wall perhaps; though not the Puerta Vieja de Bisgara, rebuilt several times over the centuries; nor at the Alcázar, completely rebuilt more than once.

In the tenth century cave that houses the Museo de la España Mágica, I stepped into a dwelling that existed when Casilda lived here. On the walls of the entrance, hands of Fatima, one of them perfectly preserved, surrounded by three elegant dark birds.

The hand of Miriam, I said out loud, touching the tiny talisman at my throat.

You have one? A Toledan example if I'm not mistaken. The museum curator smiled warmly, held out his hand. Mateo, he offered.

Miriam, I said.

Ah, I see the connection. Did you buy it here?

I shook my head. It belonged to my mother, but it was passed down to her from… a friend… another Miriam — it had been in her family since the Twenties, I think, but it's supposed to be even older.

Mateo nodded. Your Spanish is very good.

Thank you. It's thanks to my aunt, she's Czech, but an amazing linguist. And I'm glad my Spanish sounds okay — I'm going to be doing my MA in it.

In Toledo?

It was my turn to nod. I was also hoping… It would be good to get a part-time job… I mean… do you ever need… My thesis is on the intersection between alchemy, Sufism and Kabbalah. I'd love to work somewhere like this. I'll be writing a novella on Santa Casilda as part of it…

Mateo's smile widened. Well, usually we hire someone extra in the summer, or around Corpus Christi when the city fills up, but there might be a way… It wouldn't be many hours…

That would be perfect, I gushed. I don't need much. My aunt… She brought me up after my father died… my mother died when I was a baby… so Eliška, that's my aunt, took me to live with her in Prague and… she saved from when I was little, so I'd have an education fund or… I stopped, wondering why

I was blurting out my life story to a stranger who I'd already asked to employ me only moments after meeting him. Sorry, you don't need to know all this... Anyway, a few hours would be perfect... if...

He nodded, dark hair wisping around an oval face, almond eyes shimmering with amusement. She sounds like an amazing aunt. How would Friday and Saturdays sound? Or any weekday except Tuesday if Friday doesn't work. We open at 11.

Really? Wow, that's... I mean I can give you references and...

I think we can take it on trust, eh?

I fought the urge to throw my arms around him.

He held out his hand. Deal?

I shook it. Absolutely. Deal.

So why don't you take some time to look around and then, if you're not busy... We could go and have a coffee and talk about what we do?

Yes. That would be... Thank you! I can't wait to tell Eliška.

At the Church of Cristo de la Luz, the little square end of it once a mosque, Mezquita Bab al-Mardum, I came to another building Casilda might have seen, even visited, touched. Would a Muslim princess have left the Alcázar? I would have to ask Mateo.

I circled the four stone columns, stood under horseshoe arches, moved between the nine ceiling vaults gazing up at their intricate designs. I've been here before, I thought, surprising myself. I've looked up through these cusped arches, contemplated the qibla wall.

The day was warm, bright. I turned towards a faint sound, a rustle of silk on skin or air thickening in shadows beneath vaulted arches, screened from the sun's glare by panels of wooden lattice.

In the mosque gardens, trees bowed under approaching autumn, leaves shimmering, some falling; the large cedar bent to the breeze. There were no fruit trees. I remembered reading how Catherine had imagined the garden full of peaches, apricots, guava or figs. The fountain by the back wall was as empty as she had found it, yet I turned towards a sound of water against stone… a word on the breeze… *Tulaytula*.

I walked uphill towards the plaza by the Cathedral, then downhill towards my apartment on Cuesta de los Escalones, narrow lanes, cobbles underfoot. Catherine thought that the city had forgotten Casilda and I felt that too, but I was glad to have found a flat in the old mediaeval town, only a ten-minute walk from the humanities' department of the University of Castilla-La Mancha in Plaza Padilla.

In the tiny apartment I delved into an intricately carved chest, mahogany grain, scent of cedar inside, pulled out wool blankets patterned with orange arches, earthen curves, ochre spirals. It was too warm to need them yet, but I laid one over the bed, another over the sitting room sofa, to cheer the place.

Between waking and sleeping, she entered my room… not Casilda or Catherine… but a woman I struggled to recognise… though she seemed familiar… as though from an earlier dream…

I turn in the night, watch her sleep; olive skin, hair a tangle of soot and pitch. So many defeats, I think, but you have chosen me. I imagine the ram caught in the thicket, the replacement sacrifice...

Her breath catches and she turns in her sleep. Does she whisper something? I reach out, stroke her face. Her eyes open and she holds out her arms.

Remember, my darling Casilda. Remember, she says, and if you can't remember, invent...

Remember how you studied the Qu'ran from the age of five, how you heard the story of Saint Marina, were fascinated by a king's daughter who ran away to lead a contemplative's life. You learned with the wisest in the taifa, became brilliant, but remained restless, disturbed by the thought of prisoners in the palace dungeons until you took them food, heard their stories, remembered Saint Marina.

What are you carrying, princess?

The soldier blocks my passage down the steps. I shrink inside the hooded cloak, colour of night sky, lift folds of a white silk robe closer, the loaves hidden.

Roses, I say.

I feel the tremor, darkness falls on me before I've hit the ground. When I wake, the steps beneath are strewn red, the air thick with the scent of roses.

At Mezquita Bab al-Mardum the next day, air a little cooler, sky brighter, azure almost white, there was a rustle of silk, shadows congealed beneath vaulted arches. In the garden water belled against stone, whispered, *Casilda*.

A heavy clot of blood slipped between my legs. Unsteady, I glanced round. No-one. I huddled into my thin cardigan, then wrapped it around my skirt to hide the blood I felt oozing through layers of clothing, beginning the climb uphill towards the apartment, cobbles jarring, abdomen aching.

The dark-haired woman walks beside me.

Casilda fell sick, she says. Remember. It was the same illness that your mother died from when you were born. There was no way to stop the blood.

I hunched into the pain, feeling stickiness seep through my thin tights. A spasm halted me.

One of the prisoners told you about the wells of San Vicente near Briviesca in la Bureba. And so you persuaded your father to send you there to be healed, became an ascetic like Saint Marina.

I began the slow trudge again. I climbed the cobbled steps towards the studded wooden door set in rough stone that let onto the courtyard beneath my apartment.

Remember the night of your death, how you sent your spirit

across Spain to Toledo to be with your father as he passed away. Some stories say you lived to be over a hundred, but we know you died young. Perhaps neither of us stays in a body for long once the other departs.

I pushed against the heavy slats of wood, slumped onto the stairs rising from the herringboned brick floor of the courtyard, waves of nausea throbbing through me, got up and inched towards my door, my hand clammy on the metal rail.

Inside, I stood on the cool cobalt tiles of the bathroom, let water scald and saturate every sense.

Blood strewed the drain crimson, tang of iron on tongue, water searing, soothing.

A shadow pale as dust flits across a mote of light, the fragrance of roses suffusing the air. Somewhere a string is plucked, faint music—

> Al-ʿūdu qud tarannam
> Bi-abdāʾi talhīn
> Wa šaqqod al-mad ā nib
> Riyād al-basātîn

When I stepped out of the shower, the flow of blood had ceased.

Here, she says, enfolding me in a white towel. And this, she adds. She holds out a white knitted shawl that I've never seen, but know from the pages of *Casilda of the Rising Moon* and from my mother's journals. She pulls it around me. It will be a chilly night, she says, the sun's losing its power. Get under the blankets. I'll make you some mint tea.

I slid between white cotton sheets, drowsed.

When I woke, the sky was dark, sharp stars dazzled through open shutters. On the bedside table of dark wood and mother of pearl, a turquoise glass of mint tea had cooled. I put my hand to my throat, felt the silk cord of palest blue, strung with a tiny hamsa: the hand of Miriam in damascene black, silver, gold.

Crossing Over
Miriam Catherine McManus

Chapter 8

In the dream she is not herself.

She enters a yard, walls rising, blind, mute, slabbing out sky, yet its granite light dazzles... She has an urge to bolt, run back to the blanketing shadows.

She lies wounded by mortar debris, her right arm and leg blood-spattered and fragment-encrusted. She retches from pain, tries to stay conscious, looks round frantically for help. Two young men run towards her...

Blood drying on flesh... bowl of beans, scum forming on the thin liquid as it cools... A voice within chants: once there was a Moorish princess with a flow of blood that wouldn't stop... A sound cracks open the sky... the screech of a metal dragon roaring... mud in fields... once there was blood, beans, a hard bench... blood drying in a room filled with... once there was...

... there are no dates on the wall—

In this red world she is another:

A heavy clot of blood slides between her thighs.

She cries out and begins to weep.

Catherine, what is it? What can I do? I...

She looks up, sees his panic.

Ben Haddaj?

I think I might be losing the baby.

Baby? You...

She scrunches against the pain and whimpers. A trickle of blood oozes onto the floor of the strange building...

Darkness.

She is born into a myth of Moorish Iberia, a fragmentary story of a Muslim princess who becomes a saint and her unrequited lover who disappears into legend...

I died a thousand years ago, Casilda says out loud to the stars.

Twenty-three years ago, her mother, who a thousand years before had been Casilda, gave birth to her in a flow of blood—before the darkness came.

Casilda paces outside the cave, aware of the faint sweet scent of oranges, blinks as a patch of light floats before her, trailing darkness behind. And through the night air she hears Ben Haddaj's voice: *It grows dark through the sea. Through my solitude...*

The stars pulse and pain sears through her temple, clotting her vision. She feels dizzy, sees the moon throbbing at the edge of the darkness.

She pitches forward, retching, dazed... she is in a yard, a grim knot of men watch her walking towards them. They stand by a pole, a rope swaying, steps to climb...

She begins to scream into the empty land, hears Ben Haddaj say: It is an extraordinary love, Casilda. We will go through many dark clouds, but in the end... hope is always born at the same time as love.

She wakes in the cave. The winter sun haloes the entrance and the stone shines pale gold. She can taste the snow in the air, metallic as blood, soft as almond blossom. On the flat stone is a new basket of food. She pours creamy milk, cuts a sliver of yellow cheese. In the distance she watches Beatriz, sleek gold pelt over undulating muscles, making for her hunting ground.

How long is it since she left Toledo? The stones of the Alcázar shining gold under the sun's heat. Her heart is at peace.

Casilda. His voice rasps.

I'm here, Father.

I knew you'd come. There's been a scent of roses all morning, my little moon.

She kneels by his divan and holds his hand, bony and clammy. His breathing is heavier and he asks, Where are we?

We're on a lake, Father. We're sat in a crystal tower at the centre of the lake. Water flows over it, but we're inside the water, dry inside the crystal which is full of wax tapers burning yellow. We're enclosed in the beautiful water, constantly renewed, always cool, never wetting us.

A voice in a dream told me this: You've built eternal palaces, but you will not live in them long. I think my time is done, my angel.

Sleep now, she tells him.

She lies on her simple bed inside the cave.

Nearly done, Beatriz, she says as the lion curls beside her thin form. She opens her hand. Look Beatriz, it was at the cave's entrance when I came through the dream. It will come back to me one day, when my heart is once again at peace. So tiny, the black and gold and white. We are always in the act of transformation, Beatriz. You'll make sure it begins its journey, won't you?

The lion nuzzles her palm, settles beside her, and Casilda closes her fingers around the tiny damascene hamsa.

It is enough, she says.

In the morning, Gasper leaves the basket on the stone as always. He turns to descend the long path down to Buezo, but turns back, not knowing why. Peering inside the cave, hoping not to encounter the mountain lion the saint calls Beatriz. He sees only Casilda, curled small like a child, thin and still. She is too still. He moves nearer. Her skin is blue-white, cold. Her green eyes have greyed to emptiness. He pulls the blanket over her face, wipes away a tear and says a prayer.

At the entrance to the cave, on the flat rock, Beatriz is standing, head bowed. He startles and she lifts her head, yellow eyes meeting his.

She's gone, he says, surprised that he is not more afraid. I'll return with Ximeno to carry her body to the village. She'll be taken good care of.

Beatriz drops her head and moves towards him, nudges him gently back towards the body.

He tries to keep his breath steady. She will not attack him, Casilda has told him over and over.

He stands by the corpse, desperate to leave, but he can feel the lion's breath on his face, as though there is something she needs to tell him. He looks down and notices Casilda's hand, clasped tight, a tiny sliver of metal protruding. He bends and eases out the tiny hand, silver and gold filigree on black metal.

He looks into the lion's eyes. You want me to take this? I'll make sure it's returned to her people.

Beatriz seems to nod. She drops to the stone, huge paws across her head and emits a shrill screech, her mourning beginning.

Thank you, Gasper whispers, edging past her. Thank you for taking care of her.

Did She Mention My Name?

December 2016

What really happened was that I hadn't seen Nathan for ten years. Not since my father's funeral.

Trust me, Miriam you'll ace it, he said, over tapas at El Botero.

I hadn't expressed any concern over my MA studies, but he was keen to reassure me anyway. He had taken a detour from an IT conference in Madrid. I was shocked at how much he seemed to have aged and how much weight he'd put on in the last ten years.

We should order more of this black pudding, Nathan said, finishing off a large glass of Cencibel. Delicious! He looked up, grimaced, sighed.

I miss her, Miriam, he said at last.

Still? I asked, instantly wishing I hadn't said this. I mean…

I know, it's been ten years, but… God, that was a terrible year! He drained his glass, poured more from the bottle, tilting it towards me in question, but I shook my head. Losing Eliška and then... Simon... God! I don't suppose she... I mean, is she seeing anyone?

I shook my head again. She's determinedly single, I told him, but I don't think...

Of course. I know, really. It's long over. He downed his glass of wine in one long gulp. And then Simon. I should have listened to him...

Sorry?

Your dad. I didn't think he was... Well, you know how it was...

Nathan, I don't know what you mean. I'm not sure what you're saying.

Another bottle?

I'm not... I think I'd like coffee.

He stood shakily. Shit. Spanish isn't one of my languages. Perverse really. Fluent Italian, but don't suppose they'd like that... You couldn't...?

Of course I can, but they speak good English. Do you want more wine?

He nodded and I went to the counter, ordered a second bottle of Cencibel., a coffee and another plate of black pudding to mop up the alcohol.

He was like death speaking, Nathan said, before I'd properly sat down again.

I can't go on like this, he said. His voice was thin, strained.

We were sat in the kitchen at Harlech. I'd always liked it there, but that day there was this smell, like night-sweats and rotting oranges. It was just before he went on that book tour in America.

I think I will have another glass, I said, as José put the new bottle and fresh glasses on the table, giving me a sympathetic smile.

Anyway, it should be you telling me about your life, Nathan said, changing the subject.

It's fine, I already told you. My voice sounded too sharp. But I don't understand what you're talking about.

I'm not sure I know what to say. Me and Eliška weren't working. We were in the kitchen and I said something about that to your dad and he said I should come and stay in December when he got back from the States. I'd like to see you, then, he said, before... He trailed away and I said, Before what, Simon? But he just smiled. Sad smile. Rueful, you know?

Nathan gulped more wine.

We fell silent for a bit, then both of us began saying something at the same moment, trailed away again. I remember feeling ill at ease, smelling that weird odour, like dying lilies, like the scent was clinging to me. And then Simon said: I want you to give her this, Nathan. I remember saying: What? And he said again: Miriam. I want you to give this to Miriam when she's sixteen. Then he handed me a copy of *In a Place of Transformation and Dread*, a pristine hardback in a plastic wrapper. It's the proof copy. Signed. Give it to her when she's sixteen, he told me.

When? My voice was still too loud.

What do you mean?

When did my father tell you all this?

I told you, that summer, before he went to America.

Oh God, Eliška told me it wasn't my fault, but I never...

Miriam? You look really pale. Have a drink. Shall I get some water?

He told you he was going to kill himself. That's what you are telling me, isn't it, Nathan?

Well, no... I mean... yes, maybe, but not in those words... I didn't think... I...

Why didn't you say something? Do something?

I didn't think he'd... I mean... he'd been depressed before...

He told you he was going to commit suicide and you said nothing! My voice had risen further and José glanced over. I smiled at José and took a deep breath, spitting out the words quietly. Eliška said he must have got the pills in the States, but somehow... that didn't change what I thought. I've always thought it was me... that is was my fault because of what happened on the beach...

Sorry, I don't follow. What happened on the beach? Nathan leant in looking unsteady, a little green.

I thought he killed himself because of me. Because of a day when I ran away from him on the beach. You'd gone back to London. Eliška was still with us and we went for a walk. Something happened when we were walking back. Eliška was ahead of us and... it was something so small... but I ran away from him. But that wasn't the reason, was it? He'd already decided. And he'd already told you what he planned to do. And you did nothing.

I stood, testing my balance. I have to go. And I left him, staring at the wine and blood sausage, mute.

Silence gnawed into me in the apartment. I picked up my phone to call Eliška, put it down again.

Miriam! Nathan was in the street below my window. The apartment buzzer rang and I ignored it, moved into the bedroom so I couldn't hear him calling.

The next morning I found a note in the little pigeon hole beneath the courtyard stairs.

Dear Miriam

Not sure what I can say. Simon said he had to be with Casilda. He was determined to die, Miriam. I didn't take the book with me. I told him he had to see a doctor, that he could give you the book himself on your sixteenth birthday. He posted it to me just before he took the pills, with a note: *In my illness I had such strange dreams... Oh, such dreams... I dare not tell you in case you think I'm mad.*

I'm sorry to have taken so long to tell you. I'm a coward. But it wasn't you, Miriam. I do know that.

When you speak to Eliška, tell her I miss her. I don't suppose she ever mentions me, but I miss her.

Yours
Nathan

God, this is the end of the story. I can't go on, I whispered to no-one, crumpling the note.

Crossing Over
Miriam Catherine McManus

Chapter 9

She watches Beatriz keeping guard at the cave's entrance. The lion has not moved all day, did not hunt at dusk. She lays a hand on her head and bends to whisper in her ear. The cat lifts her head momentarily, then closes her eyes to sleep.

She watches the moon rising, the way the water of the spring becomes crystal white where the moonbeams fall on it.

The world is white.

She sees the tiny garden of the Mesquita Bab-al-Mardum filled with shadows. She opens her arms to embrace her futures. She whispers her name into the breeze: *Casilda* and the women turn towards her, as though she is looking into many mirrors...

And a shadow white as dust flits across a mote of moonlight and is gone, the fragrance of roses suffusing the air. Somewhere a string is plucked, faint music—

*Al-'ūdu qud tarannam
Bi-abdā'i talhın
Wa ŝaqqod al-madā nib
Riyād al-basatîn*

Fine as Fine Can Be

June 2020

Miriam tries to remember the directions. She passes the cathedral, along the wide avenue with its plazas, past the fountains and into the narrower Calle del Sepulchre and into Plaza San Bruno, the faded orange and mint plastic chairs are full with tourists and locals drinking beers and coffee in the shade of the high walls. She walks on to Calle del Deán, under ancient arches and along faceless alleyways into Calle Pabostria. In square of Calle Diego Dormer she pauses, admitting to herself that she is lost in the maze of Zaragoza's narrow streets. She follows Calle San Velero onto a wider street lined with shops, Calle Don Jaime 1, glances at her watch.

The sun is hotter now. She breathes deeply, takes out her phone and concedes to the app that will plan her route. Still 1.9 km to go. She begins to walk, overheated and impatient. But she carries the image of the apartment with her — its jewel-bright patchwork bedspread; its attic beams of aged wood and the tiled tabletop where she has placed a candle, its light desk and narrow sofa; scents of patchouli and linen.

She pauses frequently to consult the flickering blue dot on her phone. The street, parallel to the busy main artery that runs along the river, is lined with old flats in faded stages of decay. At street level, graffiti jostles between dark tabernas populated by bulging middle-aged men. She quickens her pace till she comes to a huge traffic island surrounded by a maze of pedestrian crossings. Beyond it, the old buildings give way to high-rise boxes from the 70s and 80s, ageing faster than the buildings that have stood for hundreds of years. But on her left, she glimpses the pale golden stones of Aljafería Palace through the greenery surrounding it. She crosses the road and heads into the park. Ahead of her, Casilda is sitting on a low wall of the palace, near the bridge that leads across to its towers, turrets and arches.

Casilda looks up and sees her. Miri! Casilda calls, running towards her, dark curls flying around her face. She embraces her, kisses her.

Hot, Miriam manages to say.

Casilda holds her at arm's length, laughs. You do look like a lobster, she says.

Miriam wipes a hand across her face. They had said goodbye only ten days ago when Casilda left London after travelling with her to be at the first book launch. Casilda had left to finish the sale of her mother's dance studio in Burgos while she'd continued the reading tour that has left her exhausted, yet elated.

The evening of the book launch had been a double celebration.

The woman holding out a copy of *Crossing Over* for her to sign is not only about Casilda's age, but resembles her, more than a little.

Miriam asks her name and the woman grins. I'd best spell it for you, she says in a soft Irish accent. It's S A O I R S E, pronounced

'Sairsha', Miriam completes for her.

Wow! It's rare to meet someone who can pronounce it. You won't know me, of course, but our mothers knew each other.

Miriam feels herself shiver. Your mother knew Catherine?

Not well, but my aunt and your mum were best friends, more than friends actually. I think you might even be named for her.

Miriam Jacobs?

Yes. I didn't know her, of course. She died in '89 when I was a baby, but my mum, Sarah, told me a lot about her and your mum. If you're not too busy or too exhausted after all this, we could get a coffee. There's something... Saoirse glances at the queue behind her waiting for signatures in their books. Anyway...

Miriam looks across the room to where Casilda is sitting, reading, waiting for her. Casilda looks drawn and thin still and Miriam hesitates, but then says, Yes. Yes, I'd love to. Are you okay waiting?

Saoirse grins and moves aside. Of course.

In the cafe Saoirse insists on buying the coffees and arrives back at their table with pastries as well. I've a terrible sweet tooth, she says, grinning and handing out plates of sugar glazed almond and apple confections. Couldn't resist.

They make small talk for only a few minutes before Casilda says. Our connection isn't only through Catherine and your aunt Miriam.

I know...

It's…

Saoirse and Casilda begin talking at once.

Sorry, it's just… Saoirse hesitates. That's kind of why I had to come. You'll think I'm mad but I had this dream, you see.

Dream? Casilda sits forward, alert.

That Cassie's daughter, sorry, I think she preferred Catherine? Anyway, that Catherine's daughter was with my… I'm not quite sure what we are to each other… third cousins or something removed, but you know what I mean?

Yes, Casilda says quietly. Our great-grandmothers were sisters, Marie and Hélène, so we must share a great-great-grandmother.

Saoirse nods vigorously, her mouth full of pastry. She catches crumbs and says, And somehow I knew that Catherine's daughter was with someone from my family, and how amazing is it that you're even called Casilda? Or perhaps not. I've had some weird dreams, but perhaps you think it best not go into that?

I think we'd understand, Miriam says.

I hoped you would. So… Saoirse takes a deep breath. Okay. Last year I went to Budapest. That's where the dreams started… And I had this idea. Mum told me that her mum had this little amulet, a hand of Miriam. It actually belonged to your great-grandmother, Marie, and then to your grandmother, Selene, and should have gone to your mum. Oh, and my condolences by the way.

Casilda nods thanks while Saoirse takes another breath.

But your mum left home before your gran handed it on and

somehow it came to us, to my gran, but then it got lost and… Saoirse stops. Oh, she says. It's… She peers at the hamsa Miriam is wearing. Is that…?

It's Miriam's turn to nod. It's a long story, she says, but somehow your aunt Miriam gave it to my mum and…

Gran never said. Did she know?

Yes, but not at first.

Because it always finds Casilda?

Miriam and Casilda glance at each other.

Yes, Casilda says. And, confusingly, it's Miriam who is Casilda… the original one… I just happen to have the name because my mother was fascinated with the story, but never knew why.

So I'm not going mad? Saoirse asks.

Not by our lights, Casilda says, laughing.

Well, that's something. So, to get back to my bit. While I was in Budapest I had this strong feeling that I should do something about the missing hamsa, but of course I couldn't really do much. Except one day I was in the Orthodox Synagogue, which is exquisite by the way, and they have this little shop and I found this.

Saoirse rummages in a copious bag and brings out a tiny box. It's not damascene and I know our family are Ashkenazi so your grandmother would have worshipped at the Great Synagogue. In fact, I think they were in the ghetto there during the War, but it's from somewhere she'd have known and it's so beautiful. I just had this unshakeable idea I should bring it for you, even though I didn't know how I'd ever find you.

She hands the box to Casilda, who sits very straight, breathing hard. Thank you, she whispers. Inside the box is a tiny silver hamsa with fine filigree fingers and a bright blue and red opal set in its centre. On the back, a Star of David is stamped into the silver.

It's exquisite, Casilda says, unclasping the chain to put it on.

Beautiful, Miriam adds. Thank you.

And all three of them weep and hug and promise to keep in touch.

And now, they are here in Zaragoza, where she had tried and failed to track down Ben Haddaj during the writing of her thesis and novella.

My headache has gone, she thinks.

Later, they will go back to the empty apartment, make love in the attic bed.

Whenever she's alone she still wonders if — after all — she has made Casilda up, but no — here she is. They have lived through the loss of Miriam Virág together. In the summer they will go to Prague again to see Isak and Eliška, then take the train to Budapest. It is time to get to know the place where her mother was born, Casilda has decided. The place where Catherine and Simon spent that extraordinary month when she was conceived, Miriam thinks. The place where Saoirse bought Casilda's silver hamsa.

It's so beautiful, Casilda says, as they take their time wandering through the palace, before each of them strolls in a different direction.

Miriam crosses to the east side of the north portico and stands in the doorway of the tiny Mosque, where once Ben Haddaj may have worshipped, though on her last visit she had felt nothing of him.

The printed guide tells her that the intertwined arches would once have been covered in plasterwork ornamented with plant motifs. The horseshoe archway over the mihrab on the qibla wall, pointing the way to the Kaaba in Mecca, is a small copy of the one in the Mezquita of Córdoba. The square becomes an octagon as the room rises towards a gallery of small-lobed archways inscribed with the Kufic characters of Surahs. There are more plant and geometric designs and intricate latticework that lets in a dapple of natural light. She looks towards the domed ceiling and back to the niche where…

He stands, hands raised as though in surrender, his back to her, facing the mihrab. The hood and fabric of his bernus are thrown back. His kamis, which falls to his knees, is of the same cotton as his serwal and he doesn't wear a turban, but a simple takiyya, like the Jewish yarmulke.

As she watches, she hears the clear, quiet voice. Allahu Akbar, he says as he places his right hand over his left and begins to recite the Istiftah Du'a

subhanakal-lahumma
wabihamdika watabarakas-muka wataaaala
judduka wala ilaha ghayruk.
a'auodu billaahi minash-shaytaanir rajeem
bis-millaahir rahmaanir raheem

She hears the words and knows them, and after them the Surah Al-Fatiha begins:

Bismillaahir Rahmaanir Raheem
Alhamdu lillaahi Rabbil 'aalameen

Allahu Akbar, she hears as he bends and intones three times, Subhanna Rabbiyal Adheem.

He stands and raises his arms again, still reciting, seemingly unaware that he is being watched, before prostrating himself, palms to the floor, repeating three times, Subhanna Rabbiyal A'laa. He rises to his knees and places his hands on the floor again. Even more softly he whispers, llaahumma-ghfir lee warhamnee wajburnee, warfa'nee, wa 'aafinee war'zuqnee.

O Allah, forgive me, have mercy on me, strengthen me, raise me in status, pardon me and grant me provision.

Allahu akbar, he repeats as he stands and begins again, going through the rak'ah three more times, until finally, his voice so low she can scarcely hear him:

O Allah, forgive me, have mercy on me, strengthen me, raise me in status, pardon me and grant me provision ... Hear, O Israel! The LORD is our God, the LORD is one! You shall love the LORD your God with all your heart and with all your soul and with all your might...

He turns and smiles in her direction. She feels herself shiver. Ben Haddaj half-nods, says, We will go through many dark clouds first, but one day our hearts will become peaceful, Casilda.

He lifts a hand in salute as...

Ah, there you are.

Casilda is beside her and she turns.

Miri? You look so pale. Are you okay?

Cold, she says.

But it's sweltering here, even in the shade. Are you ill?

No. No, it's just... I saw Ben Haddaj, just before he set off for Jerusalem and...

They stand on the marble floor gazing at the archway over the floodlit niche, silent.

The mezquita is empty.

Casilda leads her through cool upper rooms with their herringbone stone floors, where each square of the high ceiling is a deep indigo with rich red and gold relief work, the later motifs of the kings of Aragon. They look down across the courtyard garden, the trees thick with oranges and the finches singing, the sound of water running into the pool.

It's beautiful, Miriam whispers. I saw him about to leave. Did he know he would drown? Too late for warning Ben Haddaj, of course.

Casilda smiles. But it's not too late for Ben Haddaj now, Miri. After all, now our hearts are at peace. Casilda hugs Miriam briefly and fiercely. Let's go and find lunch before we go back to the apartment.

She cannot stop the memories, much fingered as they are.

In the white-walled flat there is laughter. Across the roofs from the window, a moonbeam path falls on the floodlit basilica.

Curled beside Casilda, Miriam drifts in almost-sleep, slips into another world:

In this beckoning place of dream, she is found.

I am Miriam, she says. She steps through a horseshoe archway, sunlight dazzling, reflecting off the little hamsa she wears at her throat. Like a star I carry with me, she thinks.

The room swells, slips back, swells forward again. She lies back on the bed, sheets crisp and cool.

In the dream, Mateo tells her she will find her lover, blesses her for the journey, knows she will succeed. Belief is your gift, a voice murmurs. She steps through another archway, longing for Casilda, a fragment of glass catches between her bare toes, one drop of blood falling onto the marble floor. Shh, a voice says. All shall be well.

She moves into the courtyard, past an enormous tree through which sun shines as though it were a thousand stars caught in the branches.

I'm here, she hears ahead of her; I'm still here.

> Vous m'avez reconnue
> Je suis la même
> Et pourtant autre

She walks towards the voice. Shadows on the wall coalesce into a film of images. She sees a boat, far out at sea, tossed, sinking, hears the noise of a train— *Just then they came in sight of thirty or forty windmills that rose from the plain...* **—the rumble of a wagon... She pitches forward, retching, dazed... She is in a yard... There is a pole, rope swaying, steps to climb... She reaches out a balancing hand... I'm still here, a voice tells her.**

Miriam wakes, sheets wound round her, rumpled.

She sits up, puts a hand out to reach Casilda, watches her sleep; olive skin, hair a tangle of soot and pitch. This isn't the end of the story, she whispers.

Casilda wakes and turns, smiles, rubs sleep from her eyes. No, she agrees. This is the beginning.

Do you still feel them with us?

Not like I used to. It's… It's like the grief has gone… and… I've lost that awful sense that I was always missing the moment.

Yes, Miriam agrees. Somehow the timing or the environment or something inside was always out of sync, but now… But… was it real? I mean… Did any of it happen?

Is that what matters? People in search of love, yearning for life to be other than it is, trying to make the world a better place. It's an eternal story. All I know is that now is the right time for us. Casilda smiles, strokes her hair. After all, Miri, until death, it's all life.

Miriam smiles, puts her arms around Casilda, whispers, For hope is always born where there is love.

Dramatis Personae

Whilst this is not an exhaustive list of characters it highlights those who reappear or have particular significance throughout the Casilda Trilogy.

from *This is the End of the Story*

Catherine McManus b.1961
> known as Cassie, she is later called Kitty by her husband and finally adopts her full name, Catherine. Her friend, Miriam, believes her to be the reincarnation of St Casilda

Miriam Jacobs b.1961
> Catherine's best friend who believes that she and Cassie have lived several lives together, most significantly as St Casilda and Ben Haddaj

Casilda (11th century)
> Moorish princess of Toledo who became a Christian saint, healer and hermit (historical figure though highly mythologised)

Ben Haddaj (11th century)
> A putative Muslim prince of Zaragoza who may have returned to his ancestral religion of Judaism (quasi-historical though largely legend)

Judith Jacobs b.1929
> Miriam Jacobs' mother.

Sarah Jacobs b.1956
> Miriam Jacob's sister

The Hamsa
> The talisman pendant, a hand of Miriam has travelled through centuries. It appears in this book in 1990 in Toledo, given to Catherine in odd circumstances.

from *A Remedy for All Things*

Selene Solweig Virág b.1927
> like Catherine, possibly an incarnation of St Casilda

Sándor Virág b.1902
> Selene's father

Marie Virág née Spire b.1903
> Selene's mother, aunt to Judith Jacobs

Hélène Spire b.1905
> Judith Jacobs' mother, aunt to Selene

Attila József 1905-1937
> Hungarian poet who committed suicide on December 3, 1937 (historical figure. The outline of his life, character & poetry is historically researched, but the events he is involved in within the novel are fictionalised, including being a possible incarnation of Ben Haddaj)

Miriam Virág b.1955
> Selene's daughter, who Selene believes is fathered by Attila József, despite the poet having died in 1937

Simon Garrett b. 1963
> Catherine's partner, possibly an incarnation of Ben Haddaj

The Hamsa
> The talisman pendant, a hand of Miriam has travelled through centuries. It appears in this book in 1924, given to Marie Spire (who becomes Marie Virág) on her 21st birthday during a family trip to Toledo

from *For Hope is Always Born*

Miriam McManus b.1994
    Catherine and Simon's daughter, possibly an incarnation of St Casilda (so present-day Miriam may be the 'historical' Casilda)

Casilda Feartes b.1988
    Selene's granddaughter and Miriam Virág's daughter, possibly an incarnation of Ben Haddaj (so present-day Casilda may be the 'quasi-historical Ben Haddaj)

Simon Garrett b. 1963
    Catherine's partner & Miriam McManus' father, possibly an incarnation of Ben Haddaj

Miriam Virág b.1955
    Selene's daughter & Casilda Feartes' mother

Casilda (11th century)
    Moorish princess of Toledo who became a Christian saint, healer and hermit (historical figure though highly mythologised) and in this book the central character of Miriam McManus' novella, *Crossing Over*.

Nathan Garrett b. 1958
    Simon's brother and Miriam McManus' uncle

Eliška Baroch b.1960
    Simon's colleague in Prague who marries his brother, Nathan & is Miriam McManus' aunt

Rafael Faertes b.1952
    Miriam Virág's partner and Casilda Faertes' father, who she does not meet

Isak Löwenthal b.1956
    Miriam Virág's later partner and Casilda Faertes' stepfather

Saoirse Jacobs Ó Murcháin b.1988
    Sarah Jacobs' daughter and Miriam Jacob's niece. Also Casilda Faertes' third cousin

Beatriz
: A mountain lion and companion to St Casilda

The Hamsa
: The talisman pendant, a hand of Miriam has travelled through centuries. It appears in this book in the early 11th century in a cave near Briviesca

Acknowledgments

The following books, websites and interviews were valuable background reading:

Quotations from and allusions to *Don Quixote* by Miguel de Cervantes are from the Gutenberg Project edition, translated by John Ormsby.

The poem fragment:

> Al-'ūdu qud tarannam
> Bi-abdā'i talhīn
> Wa ṣaqqod al-mad ā nib
> Riyād al-basātîn

[The lute began to resound with the most beautiful melodies, and the brooks flowed gaily through the flower gardens.]
is from *Hispano-Arabic Poetry; an Anthology*, translated by James T Monroe, Gorgias Press.

The Biblical quotations (The Shema Yisrael, Deut. 6:4-5 & the De Profundis, Psalm 130:1) are from the New Revised Standard Version Bible, copyright © 1989 the Division of Christian Education of the National Council of the Churches of Christ in the United States of America. Used by permission. All rights reserved.

There are several websites in English and Spanish with competing but sketchy accounts of the life of Casilda. I have taken my inspiration from several sources and added my own interpretations, but am grateful to Elizabeth Borton de Trevino's children's novel, *Casilda of the Rising Moon*, Penguin, 1967, which I first read in 1972.

Similarly, there are many websites, books and monographs on the links between Sufi philosophy and Kabbalah. I have used sources creatively and loosely but am grateful to:

> Tom Block, 'The Question of Sufi Influence on the Early Kabbalah' in *Sophia: The Journal of Traditional Studies*, Oakton, VA, Winter, 2007-2008;

A S Halkin, 'The Judeo-Islamic Age,' in *Great Ages and Ideas of the Jewish People*, ed. Leo Schwarz, (New York: Random House, 1956);

Scholem Gershem, *Origins of the Kabbalah*, (New Jersey: The Jewish Publication Society, 1987);

Joseph Dan and Ronald Kiener, *The Early Kabbalah* (intro), (Mahweh, NJ: Paulist Press, 1986).

The titles of the chapters mirror those in *This is the End of the Story* and are taken from song titles by the Canadian folk singer, Gordon Lightfoot.